KALLOCAIN

Library of World Fiction

Kallocain
Karin Boye
Translated from the Swedish by Gustaf Lannestock

The Werewolf
Aksel Sandemose
Translated from the Norwegian by Gustaf Lannestock

KALLOCAIN

BY KARIN BOYE

TRANSLATED FROM THE SWEDISH
BY GUSTAF LANNESTOCK
WITH AN INTRODUCTION
BY RICHARD B. VOWLES

THE UNIVERSITY OF WISCONSIN PRESS

The University of Wisconsin Press
1930 Monroe Street, 3rd floor
Madison, Wisconsin 53711-2059
uwpress.wisc.edu

3 Henrietta Street
London WC2E 8LU, England
eurospanbookstore.com

Printed in the United States of America

Library of Congress Cataloging-in-Publication Data
Boye, Karin, 1900–1941
Kallocain / Karin Boye ;
translated by Gustaf Lannestock; with an introduction by Richard B. Vowles.
(Library of world fiction.)
Originally published by Albert Bonniers Förlag AB, Stockholm, Sweden
ISBN 0-299-03894-7 (pbk.: alk. paper)
Library of Congress Catalog Card Number 66-13798

ISBN-13: 978-0-299-03894-6 (pbk: alk. paper)

Karin Boye's literary successes lie at opposite ends of a spectrum reaching from the private to the public and, in another sense, from a mythical past to a hypothetical future. Hers is the victory of extremity. She will be remembered for two books, the collected poetry, numbering some three hundred pages, and *Kallocain* (1940), which deserves to take a secure place in the literature of dystopia, among such novels as Aldous Huxley's *Brave New World* and George Orwell's *1984*. Her works reflect, on the one hand, a lyrical inwardness and, on the other, an oracular sense of public responsibility. It was Karin Boye's tragedy that the two fields lay hopelessly apart. There was, to return to the original image, no sure continuity of the spectrum.

Though rarely time-bound, Karin Boye belongs to the literary twenties and thirties. To American readers, she will seem most easily associated with Pär Lagerkvist, who made his debut in 1912, and Harry Martinson, who appeared on the scene in 1929. All three are melodic poets making sacrament of simple things, though Boye's yearning for the ideal sets her somewhat apart. All three, interestingly enough, ventured into the chill realms of dystopia. "The Children's Campaign," which Lagerkvist published in 1935, studies the grim mechanism and bloody combat of a totalitarian youth corps in a fashion that obviously had a partial influence on *Kallocain*. Martinson ultimately came to create a significant merger of poetry and science fiction in *Aniara,* the symbolic story of a way-ward space ship, now widely known as an opera by Carl-Birger Blomdahl. But both Lagerkvist and Martinson are more robust, more resilient. They were able to mend cleavages of the soul and lesions of the heart. They have survived, and they continue to write. Still, Karin Boye will live as a poignancy and an intensity of some moment in Swedish letters.

II

Karin Boye was born in 1900 in the shipping and industrial city of Göteborg. The daughter of a civil engineer of German descent, she grew up in a home environment that was both religious and intellectual. Her early ecstasies over now Christ now Nietzsche might not have been brought into dangerous conflict had she not been sent at the age of twenty to a seminary where she encountered a hardened, institutionalized Christianity that seemed to efface her life impulses, her real identity. The resultant emotional upheaval is documented in the series of Socratic dialogues published under the title of *Crisis* (*Kris,* 1934), a book in which the two sides of her personality are represented by Malin Forst I and Malin Forst II, and sometimes further abstracted into the chess pieces Black and White—standing for the Dionysian and the Apollonian, the instinct and the intellect.

When Karin Boye went to Uppsala University in 1922, to continue her studies, her first volume of poetry, *Clouds* (*Moln*), had just appeared. Her life continued to be a series of crises. She joined the international worker movement Clarté, which enjoyed a more sustained dedication in Sweden than in any other European country except France, the native country of its founder, Henri Barbusse. It would be difficult to locate Karin Boye's precise ideological position between social democracy and communism, but suffice it to say that she was actively engaged in Clarté until a 1928 trip to Russia brought disillusionment. Then and in the early thirties she wrote extensively for the liberal journals and the little magazines, chiefly *Spektrum*, which did so much to acquaint Sweden with the surrealists and T. S. Eliot. She and the critic-librarian Erik Mesterton, then a fellow writer for *Spektrum*, made the very fine Swedish translation of *The Waste Land*.

An early, unsuccessful marriage to an Uppsala Clartéist was the first of several emotional defeats that finally led Karin Boye to seek psychoanalytic help in Berlin. She continually sought therapy there and in Sweden and, while the experience fructified her prose works and to some degree colored her poetry, it accomplished nothing for her permanent peace of mind. In 1941, in a land strangely sequestered from the hates of Europe, she walked out into the night and took her own life.

Two volumes of poetry, *Hidden Country* (*Gömda land*, 1924), and *Hearths* (*Härdarna*, 1927), followed *Clouds* and established Boye's reputation as a poet before the end of the twenties. But her full and exciting maturity came only with the volume *For Love of the Tree* (*För trädets skull*), which appeared in 1935. It is customary to see new promise in "The Seven Deadly Sins" ("De sju dödsynderna"), a fragment of a cantata, and other posthumously published poems; but it strikes me that resignation and defeat had begun to damp the vitality of her poetic impulse. Nevertheless, the poetry has the flexibility and assurance of Eliot's *Murder in the Cathedral*, from which it clearly derived a measure of inspiration.

In 1931, as if to meet the social demands of a new decade, Karin Boye made her debut in prose. To the surprise of the critics who had pigeon-holed her as a poet, she won a major Scandinavian book award with *Astarte*, a book impressive for its "living, natural, and infallibly sure prose," [1] but somewhat removed from novelistic orthodoxy. It is, by virtue of an irony which Boye seems to have reserved for her prose, an expressionistic portrayal of city mores, presided over after a fashion by the goddess Astarte, who has been metamorphosed from her Asiatic splendor into a gilded, smirking window mannequin.

In *Merit Wakens* (*Merit vaknar*, 1933) Boye accomplishes a fractional distillation of love. A widow discovers that her husband was far from the man she thought him to be, that he had in fact embezzled and was being blackmailed at one time. The spectacle of a young couple whose relationship is about to collapse convinces the disillusioned widow that sacrifices have to be made for love and that she must cherish her husband's memory for what it was. Love has to be accepted conditionally, as it were. *Too Little* (*För lite*, 1936) is Karin Boye's version of the poet trapped in a prosaic marriage, unable to realize himself in poetry or in love. Undoubtedly these two realistic novels come close to the problems of Boye's own life.

Kallocain, which appeared in the fall of 1940, was immediately greeted as the finest of Karin Boye's novels. "Of international class," wrote Artur Lundkvist; and Karl Ragnar Gierow did not hesitate to call it "a significant and lasting work of art." [2] This sinister vision of a world state might well be described as a montage of what Karin Boye had seen or surmised in Soviet Russia and Nazi Germany. In it she absolves herself of any lingering stigma of political naïveté.

It is possible to admire Karin Boye's prose for its color, texture, and precision, but by and large fiction was not her medium. The truth is that she did not know people well

[1] Sten Selander, quoted in the introduction to *Astarte* (Bonnier, 1949), p. 42.

[2] Quoted in the introduction to *Kallocain* (Bonnier, 1949), pp. xiv–xv.

enough to have any real gift for characterization. The figures in her novels are either extensions of herself, fragments from a mirror that was never one whole, placid surface; or they are abstract poles sparking her troubled, tortured dialectic. She could not project her emotions so well into people as into things; and the investing of object and form with emotional content is much more the concern of poetry.

III

The lyricism of Karin Boye is so intensely personal that it seems neither very Swedish nor very modern. Except for the images of ice and cold, a fleeting preoccupation with the Uppsala plains, and the rare appearance of the mythical *Æsir* (gods) and the *álfar* (elves), Scandinavian scenes and personages are notably absent from her poetry. The world of Boye's poetry is the world of self; it subsists on its own almost confessional vibrancy. The lyric strain may be narrow, but it has depth and a kind of liquid purity. To read much modern poetry is to go by train, absorbing all the shocks, glimpsing the sordid and the lovely alike, the billboards, the festoons of laundry, the ideographs of smoke besmirching the sky, the sweet and desperate faces, the rich, colliding color. To read the poetry of Karin Boye is to force oneself Alastor-like up the river of the soul, where a torment of vegetation thrusts back a somber sky, where all nature is reflection of the poet's mind, a vista of the poet's anguish.

Or, the poetry of Karin Boye might be described as an ascent to symbolic fulfillment, through anguish and pain:

> I am sick from poison. I am sick from a thirst
> for which nature has provided no healing drink.
>
> Rivulets and springs flow everywhere;
> I kneel to take the sacrament of the earth's veins.

And holy rivers inundate the heavens. I lean back,
feel my lips wet with white ecstasies.

But nowhere, nowhere . . .

I am sick from poison. I am sick from a thirst
for which nature has provided no healing drink.

Karin Boye is something of the saint thirsting in the desert; she is, in fact, *drabbad av renhed* (beset by, scourged by purity), in the phrase from the poem "Cherubim" which Margit Abenius chose as the trenchant title of her Karin Boye biography. In that poem, the image of "beast-angels . . . with lion feet and sun wings" is expressive of the struggle between body and soul that plagued her from early seminary days.

Boye's rejection of reality is Platonic with mystical overtones. In the early poem "Idea" she sees herself as a "lying mirror image"; later her vision has a kind of Blakean ecstasy:

The world is dreamed by a sleeping god,
and the quivering dawn waters his soul.
Memories of things that happened yesterday,
before the world was;
ghosts, glimpses.

In the search for adequate defense against the world of actuality, Karin Boye musters images of cleansing, excision, hardness, and armored protection. Truth, for her, must be cold steel, the surgeon's knife. She would don a coat of mail, very like that of the Christian crusader. But finally her militancy dissolves into images of softness and sensitivity as more suitable to a philosophy of love. Hers is a pagan variant of Eliot's "Teach me to care and not to care, / Teach me to sit still."

The wonderfully expansive, luminous symbols of *For Love of the Tree* make it the pinnacle of Karin Boye's achievement. "The deep violoncello of night casts its dark rejoicing over the expanses," she sings, and of another hour, "Blond morning lay your lambent hair against my cheek." The poet is both mother and microcosm:

> Ripe as a fruit the world lies in my bosom
> it has ripened overnight
> and the rind is the thin blue film
>   that tightens bubble-round
> and the juice is the sweet and fragrant,
>   running, burning
>   flood of sunlight.

"Ripeness is all," the poet might say in the words of Shakespeare's Edgar.

Indeed a kind of vegetant harmony informs the best of Boye's poetry and the tree is her most expressive symbol. Growth is for her both cruel and wonderful. "Of course it hurts when buds are bursting," she confesses, but she will pray for a rooted existence, for hands that burst open like flowers. She would be Yeats's "great rooted blossomer," not "bruising body to pleasure soul." Karin Boye and Virginia Woolf have often been called kindred spirits, for scarcely more reason than that their deaths were similar immolations; but Boye is closer to Katherine Mansfield in pathos and symbolic statement. One thinks of the pear tree in "Bliss" and Mansfield's outburst in a letter of May 1919: "O this spring—it makes me *long* for happiness. . . . Why are human beings the only ones who do not put forth fresh buds—exquisite flowers and leaves? I cannot bear to go among them." [3]

The tree comprehends all; Boye loves its organic assurance, its oneness—and its magic possibility as symbol:

> A tree grows beneath the earth;
> an hallucination haunts me,
> a song of living glass, of burning silver.
> Like darkness before light
> all weight must melt
> and only one drop of song fall from the leaves.

[3] *Letters*, ed. J. M. Murry (Albatross, 1938), p. 164.

An anguish consumes me.
It seeps from the earth.
A tree writhes in the heavy layers of earth.
O wind! Sunlight!
Feel this agony:
the promise of a breath of paradise below.

Here and elsewhere the tree takes on mythic identity; it is Ygdrasil, the tree of life, as well as the tree of the poet's life. It is, however, no intellectual totem, consciously adopted because of its ubiquity as a cultural symbol. Rather, it seems to spring from the "collective unconscious"; it is the poet's bond with the fecund earth, with the racial past, present, and future.

It might even be said that Karin Boye's lyric development describes a vegetative cycle. Her early poetry is a sapling: lean, sinuous, and possessed of a hymnlike simplicity (one thinks of such lines as "Unlocked the copper portal of the world," "I know a path that takes me home," "Your every word is like a seed," "The onetime said is forever said," and "I am a priest of poverty"); then comes efflorescence and a rich harvest of symbols. Finally the tree has gained in strength and dignity but lost its former glow; the later poetry is firmly rooted, its limbs are raised in the posture of supplication so typical of Boye, but one senses inevitably the "drift toward death."

And so life ends in a quasi-mystic resignation. Karin Boye might recognize the possibility of two gods, "the god we create, and the god who creates us—the one within us and in the world's will"; but she would have only the latter god, a god who was "a dark, shaping power, behind and beyond the visible, always in flux and animation . . . a just, inspiriting star glance," as Margit Abenius has put it.[4] It was a god who brought Boye's poetry to the kind of symbolic fruition I have attempted to describe, but gave

[4] Introduction to *Dikter* (Bonnier, 1942), p. 8.

spiritual solace in no sufficient measure. Karin Boye's final vision is concentrated in the brief, but lovely, "Dark Angels," one of her last poems:

> The dark angels with blue flames
> like flowers of fire in their black hair
> know the answers to strange, blasphemous questions—
> and perhaps they know where the bridge is
> from the depths of night to the light of day—
> and perhaps they know the guise of all unity—
> and there may be in our final home
> a bright dwelling that bears their name.[5]

IV

Kallocain was written during the summer of 1940, less than a year before Karin Boye's suicide. The task was pure torture partly because she had never attempted to hold together so large a book "without an ounce of autobiography" and partly because the very subject filled her with increasing terror. When she submitted the finished manuscript to her publisher on 21 August, she wrote: "I know well enough that the novel has its failings, but at least it is exciting, and, if it's any consolation, I promise that I shall never write anything so macabre again." And she added: "In any case, it was something I had to do." Though she readily admitted the influence of her recent reading in Kafka, she seemed, perhaps in whimsy, to imply some outside instrumentality. To the compliments of her mother, she replied: "Do you really think it was *I* who did it?" [6]

Kallocain is the first-person account of Leo Kall, a scientist in the totalitarian Worldstate, who has discovered a truth serum of disarmingly pale green color, which, when injected into the bloodstream, reduces the inhibition

[5] Translated by Alan Blair, *Life and Letters,* 63 (October 1949), 21. All other translations are my own.
[6] Quoted in Margit Abenius, *Karin Boye* (Aldus, 1965), pp. 296–97.

threshold and compels the patient to blurt out the whole truth. His drug is of inestimable value to the police state because it eliminates the last vestige of privacy. It fulfills the prognostication of Dostoevsky's Grand Inquisitor, the patron saint of all dystopias:

> And they will have no secrets from us. We shall allow or forbid them to live with their wives or mistresses, to have or not to have children—according to whether they have been obedient or disobedient—and they will submit to us gladly and cheerfully. The most painful secrets of their conscience, all, all they will bring to us, and we shall have an answer for all. And they will be glad to believe our answer, for it will save them from the great anxiety and terrible agony they endure at present in making a free decision for themselves.[7]

In the world of *1984*, "nothing was your own except the few cubic centimeters inside your skull," but that too must become a property of the Worldstate. Karin Boye probably knew very little about pentothal and sodium amytal, though she might have heard of them through her friend, Ebbe Linde, the chemist turned poet and critic. Rumors of truth drugs and various forms of chemical persuasion were already current in the 1940's.

Kallocain, named after the drug, is the confession of a dedicated party member turned deviationist. "Confession" is perhaps too strong a word, because the narrative is notably matter-of-fact and emotionless (*kall* means both "cold" and "profession" in Swedish). The style reflects the imprint of a society reduced to austerity and routine. But when Kall experiences conversion, the style gains resonance as the lost values reassert themselves.

Dr. Kall's chief wish, so he believes, is to be a "good fellow-soldier, a happy, healthy cell in the state organism." "From individualism to collectivism," he says, "from

[7] *The Brothers Karamazov* (Everyman, 1950), p. 265. See D. Richards, "Four Utopias," *The Slavonic and East European Review,* 40 (1961), 220.

aloneness to communion, such had been the course of this giant, holy organism in which the individual was only a cell. . . . Kallocain was a necessary stage in this whole development, since it widened the communion to encompass the inner self, which had been kept private before." Kall moves up the power ladder by testing the drug on many human guinea pigs and then persuading the police that Kallocain might be of use to them.

Kall is, however, troubled by memories of another communion than that of the State. He remarks, "One might speak of 'love' as an obsolete, romantic concept, but I am afraid it exists anyway, and from its very inception it contains an indescribably painful element." He has these vestigial feelings for his wife Linda—beautiful, strong, uncommunicative—and desperately unhappy. To him she has become a frightening and almost hateful enigma.

But even more disturbing to Leo Kall's peace of mind is his immediate superior in the laboratory, Edo Rissen. It is not simply that Leo Kall, a petty Othello of the test-tube kind, suspects his wife of previous infidelities with Rissen. It is that they have something in common that he has not, something that perhaps he once had. Rissen is too casual, too lax, too permissive—in short, too humane. He has an inner core of security that protects him from the multiple terrors in the power struggle of the State. He is, in other words, suspect as a fellow-soldier and a throw-back to the "Civilian Era." In the thought-controlled society of the Worldstate, Rissen observes sagely but without a trace of smug phrase-making: "No fellow-soldier over forty can have a clear conscience."

This is, of course, why citizens over the age of ten had to be deported from Plato's Republic and the past had to be systematically eradicated in the society of 1984. History is heresy.

Leo Kall, approaching forty, caught up in the State's

network of mutual suspicion, and running short on tranquilizers, strikes out at his imagined adversaries. He performs a kind of mental rape on Linda, with some Kallocain smuggled out of the laboratory. Disappointed in the results, he brings about the arrest and subsequent trial of Rissen.

As for Linda, after the shock of the Kallocain injection, she decides she has a choice, either to kill Leo or to make a gift of her complete confidence, to open her heart and mind to him altogether. She chooses the latter course, and he is transfigured by the discovery that there *is* a higher communion and a stronger attachment possible than that of individual and State. Liberated from fear, he tries to save Rissen, recognizing that his strong feeling toward that strange man is closer to love than to hate.

But there is no turning back. Others were bound to inform on a man like Rissen, and they have. Indeed, Leo sees neither wife nor rival again. Nor his three children, who in any case belonged more to the state than to him. Kall's role in the Worldstate ends abruptly when he is captured by a raiding party from the enemy Universal State. It is only after twenty years of captivity (a life not very different, as he remarks, from his erstwhile "freedom") that he undertakes to write down his "memories of a certain eventful time" in his life.

The usual dystopian conditions prevail in the Worldstate. The state is everything, the individual is nothing, regulation prevails, and that which cannot be regulated is outlawed or extirpated. The focal character occupies a position of ambiguity and indecision between the old and new. He is sufficiently sensitive to observe and report change, but he is numb and impotent. Ultimately he is assimilated or destroyed by the new order of society. On the other hand, this is not to say that *Kallocain* is like all other dystopian fiction.

In *Brave New World,* written some nine years before, the race of man has been conditioned by prenatal treatment and postnatal suggestion into a vacuous euphoria which is maintained by booster doses of *soma.* Huxley's novel, with its Social Predestination Room, its feelies, its songs ("Orgy-porgy, Ford and fun"), and characters like Helmholtz Watson, Bernard Marx, and Mustapha Mond, displays all the comic inventiveness of the musical revue. If Huxley chose to laugh a technological world out of countenance, Karin Boye found the strangulation of all individuality too devastating to laugh at. *Kallocain* is not satire, although the flat understatement of Leo Kall's chronicle may constitute a minor irony of method. The names sound like the coinages of science fiction. While some are identifiably Greek (Kalipso Lavris), Japanese (Kakumita), and Hamitic (Tuareg), most of them are vaguely Baltic in sound. At any rate, they are not chosen for their comic possibility.

George Orwell's *1984,* which appeared eight years after *Kallocain,* is at the same time both more sophisticated and less sophisticated than Karin Boye's dystopia. It documents the philosophy of the world state in far more detail, but it keeps physical torture as an instrumentality of the state, when subtler methods of persuasion are available. So *1984* is both novel-of-idea and melodrama, and it may be argued whether the two are entirely compatible. Karin Boye, on the other hand, is concerned with one man's mind, a scientific mind, and perhaps therefore a politically naïve mind, as it documents its past life in the hallucinatory horror of the Worldstate. Ideology and police violence, while they exist, fall outside the perimeter of her fiction.

The closest relative and very likely the progenitor of *Kallocain* was yet another and earlier fantasy, *We* (1920), by Eugene Zamiatin, the self-styled "devil of Soviet literature." [8] In this case the hero-narrator D-503 is a mathematician who designed the *Integral*, a space ship which, "like a flaming Tamerlane of happiness," will visit other planets and bring all beings into the fold of the United State. It will unbend the last wild curve, "integrate the colossal universal equation."

Like Leo Kall, D-503 is caught between two worlds. Although a zealot of the new life of reason, he conducts an old-style clandestine love affair, no easy feat in his glass city, and as a result he is caught up in a revolutionary movement. Finally he submits to official lobotomy and, already depersonalized, he now joins the happy deactivated masses of the state. Always there is some inner cancer to be excised. In *We* it is fancy, or imagination; in *1984*, it is memory; in *Kallocain* it is the *élan vital*, the hidden well-spring of love.[9] For love is the stubborn center of man and the most difficult to remove.

The symbolic use of *green* is important to both novels. Defying the United State means penetrating the Green Wall that surrounds it. Moving to a secret rendezvous, D-503 writes:

> From beyond the Wall, from the infinite ocean of green, there arose toward me an immense wave of roots, branches, flowers, leaves. It rose higher and higher and higher; it seemed as though it would splash over me and that from a man, from the finest and most precise mechanism which I am, I would be transposed into . . .[10]

D-503 does not dare finish the sentence; but Edo Rissen, under the influence of the truth serum, expresses his faith in somewhat similar terms of color:

> I wanted so to believe there was a green depth in the human being, a sea of undefiled growth-power that melted all dead remnants in its crucible and healed and created in eternity . . .

[8] Peter Rudy, "Introduction," *We* (Dutton paperback, 1952), p. vi.
[9] Cf. D. Richards, p. 226.
[10] *We*, p. 88.

Typically Karin Boye, in moments of intensity, resorts to the symbols of her poetry. Beneath the concrete expanses of the Worldstate lies the source spring of her lyricism. "The objective world-image, the logical-scientific, is a gridwork we stretch over our personal experiences," she wrote in the essay "Language Beyond Logic." [11] If Karin Boye subjugates or sublimates the poet in herself in *Kallocain*, it is to demonstrate that much more dramatically how the gridwork of reason can become a world prison and how it can bring about the death of the self.

RICHARD B. VOWLES

December, 1965

[11] "Språket bortom logiken," *Spektrum* (1932), reprinted in *Tendens och verkan* (Bonnier, 1949), p. 42.

BY KARIN BOYE

All of Karin Boye's works were published by Albert Bonnier, Stockholm, Sweden.

POETRY

Moln (*Clouds*). 1922.
Gömda land (*Hidden Country*). 1924.
Härdarna (*Hearths*). 1927.
För trädets skull (*For Love of the Tree*). 1935.
"De sju dödssynderna" ("The Seven Deadly Sins"). 1940, but unpublished until its appearance in *Dikter*.
Dikter (*Poems*). 1942.

PROSE

Astarte (*Astarte*). 1931. Novel.
Merit Vaknar (*Merit Wakens*). 1933. Novel.
Uppgörelser (*Reckonings*). 1934. Short stories.
Kris (*Crisis*). 1934. Novel.
För lite (*Too Little*). 1936. Novel.
Ur funkton (*Out of Commission*). 1940. Short stories.
Kallocain (*Kallocain*). 1940. Novel.
Bebådelse (*Annunciation*). 1941. Stories and sketches.

Samlade skrifter (*Collected works*). 1948–49.
"Det öde landet." 1932. A translation with Erik Mesterton of T. S. Eliot's *The Waste Land*. In *Dikter i urval*, ed. Ronald Bottrall and Erik Mesterton. Stockholm: Bonnier, 1942.

Abenius, Margit. *Drabbad av renhed.* Stockholm: Bonnier, 1950. Reprinted from the third edition (1956) as a paperback under the title *Karin Boye,* Bonnier Aldusbok A-122, 1965.

————. "De sju dödssynderna," in *Kontakter.* Stockholm: Bonnier, 1944.

———— and Olof Lagercrantz, eds. *Karin Boye: minnen och studier.* Stockholm: Bonnier, 1942.

Bergen, Eskil. *Clarté: poeter och politiker.* Stockholm: Bonnier, 1945.

Bergstrand, Maja. "Med hednisk tendens," *Bonniers litterära magasin,* 7 (1938), 112–19.

Gustafson, Alrik. *A History of Swedish Literature.* Minneapolis: University of Minnesota Press, 1961. Pp. 467–69, 636.

Harrie, Ivar. *In i fyrtiotalet.* Stockholm: Bonnier, 1944. Pp. 332–43.

Jaensson, Knut. "Karin Boye," in *Nio moderna svenska prosaförfattare.* Stockholm: Bonnier, 1941. Pp. 62–66.

Kjellén, Alf. "Havssymbolik hos Karin Boye: en utvecklingslinje i hennes 20-talsdiktning," in *Studier tillägnade Henry Olsson.* Stockholm: 1956. Pp. 296–313.

Richards, S. "Four Utopias," *The Slavonic and East European Review,* 40 (1961), 220–28.

Stolpe, Sven. "Karin Boye," in *Kämpande dikt.* Stockholm: Kooperativa förbundets bokförlag, 1938. Pp. 19–29.

Vowles, Richard B. "Ripeness Is All: A Study of Karin

Boye's Poetry," *Bulletin of the American Swedish Institute*, 7 (1952), 3–8. My introduction is a revision and an expansion of this article.

Walsh, Chad. *From Utopia to Nightmare*. London: Geoffrey Bles, 1962.

KALLOCAIN

The book I now sit down to write must seem pointless to many—if indeed I dare imagine "many" will have the opportunity to read it—since of my own volition, without anyone's request, I undertake such a work, and since I myself am not quite clear as to the purpose. I must and will, that's all. The demand for purpose and method in one's doings and sayings has become more and more exacting, lest a single word might be uttered haphazardly; but the author of this book has been forced to take the opposite course, out into purposelessness, because even though my years here as prisoner and chemist—they must be more than twenty, I suppose—have been well enough filled with work and urgency, there is a something that feels this to be insufficient and that has inspired and envisioned another labor within me, one which I myself could not have envisioned, and in which I nevertheless have been deeply and almost painfully involved. That labor will be completed when I have finished my book. Consequently, I realize how unreasonable and irrational my scribblings must seem in comparison to all rational and practical thinking; yet write I must.

Perhaps I would not have dared earlier. Perhaps it is simply that my imprisonment has made me heedless. My living conditions now differ only slightly from those I had as a free man. The food might have been a shade poorer here; I soon got accustomed to that. The mattress appeared to be a little harder than my bed at home in

Chemistry City No. 4; I adjusted to that. I was permitted into the fresh air more seldom; this also I grew accustomed to. Worst was the separation from my wife and children, especially as I knew nothing, nor do now, about their fate; this filled me with uneasiness and apprehension during my first years of imprisonment. But gradually, as time passed, I began to feel more calm even than before and felt ever more at home with my existence. Here I have nothing to worry about, neither subordinates nor chiefs—with the exception of the prison guards, who seldom disturb me in my work and are only concerned about my obeying the rules. I have neither protector nor competitor. The scientists who have been introduced to me from time to time, to keep me up to date with what is new in chemistry, have always treated me pleasantly and with a matter-of-fact attitude, even though perhaps somewhat condescendingly because of my foreign nationality. I know that no one has reason to envy me. In short: in a way I can feel freer than in freedom. But at the same time as my calm increased, this strange connection with my past grew within me, and now I will have no peace until I have written down my memories of a certain eventful time in my life. The opportunity to write has been given me on account of my scientific work, and there is no inspection before the moment I submit a completed task. Consequently I am able to afford myself this pleasure, even though it might be my last.

At the time my story begins I was approaching forty. If any further introduction is necessary perhaps I might mention the way I symbolized life. Few things tell more about a person than his life-symbol: whether he sees it as a road, a great battle, a growing tree, or a billowing sea. For my part I looked at it, with the eyes of an obedient schoolboy, as a staircase on which one had to rush from level to level as fast as one could, short of breath, one's competitor at one's heels. Yet I had in reality very few competitors. Most of my colleagues at the laboratory concentrated their ambitions towards the military field and considered our daily work a boring but necessary interruption of the evening's military exercises. As for myself, I would hardly have dared admit to anyone of them how much greater was my interest in my chemistry than in my military participation, even though I was far from a poor soldier. Anyway, I was rushing ahead up my staircase. How many steps I actually had to put behind me I had never thought about, nor what kind of glory awaited me at the top. Perhaps I vaguely imagined life's house as one of our ordinary city dwellings, underground, where one emerged from the earth's bowels and at last reached the roof terrace, in open air, in wind and daylight. What wind and daylight might correspond to in my life-course was not quite clear to me. But certain it was that each new staircase level was indicated by short, official notices from higher authorities: a successful examination, a passed test, a promotion to some more important field of activity. I had already behind me many such important points of beginning and completion, though not so many that a new one would seem less important. It was therefore with a touch of exhilaration that I returned from the short telephone conversation which had advised me that I could expect my control-chief the following day, and consequently would begin to experiment with human material. Tomorrow, then, would come the final ordeal by fire for my greatest discovery up to that time.

I felt in such high spirits it seemed difficult for me to start anything new during the ten minutes still left of my working period. Instead I cheated a little—for the first time in my life, I believe—and began to put away paraphernalia too early, slowly and cautiously, while glancing through the glass partitions on either side to see if anyone was watching me. As soon as the signal bell announced that the day's work was over I hurried out into the long laboratory corridors, one of the first in the rush. Quickly I took my shower, changed my work clothes for the leisure-time uniform, jumped into the elevator and in a few moments was standing on the street above. Since our apartment had been allotted in my working district, I had been granted a surface permit there, and I always enjoyed stretching a little out in the open.

As I passed the Metro-station it occurred to me I might as well wait for Linda. Since I was so early she could not as yet have got home from her provision factory, a good twenty-minute subway ride away. A train had just arrived and a flood of human beings welled up out of the earth, pressed through the turnstiles where their surface permits were checked, and spread through the streets all around me. Standing there watching this swarm of humanity, these homeward bound fellow-soldiers in leisure-time uniform—the roof terraces in the background empty now except for the rolls of mountain-gray and meadow-green canvas which in ten minutes could make the city invisible from the air—it struck me suddenly that perhaps all these individuals harbored the same dream as I: the dream of the way up.

The thought stirred me. I knew that in days gone by, during the Civilian Era, it had been necessary to entice people to effort and work through hope for roomier living quarters, better food, and more attractive dress. Nowadays nothing of this sort was required. The standard apartment—one room for unmarried, two for a family— was sufficient for all, from the lowest to the most deserving. The food of the establishment satisfied the top general as well as the private. The common uniform—one for work, one for leisure, and one for military and police service—was the same for all, for men and women, for high and low, except for the insignia. This last was actually no fancier for one than for another. The desirability of higher insignia lay purely in what it symbolized. I thought happily, so highly spiritualized is actually every fellow-soldier in the Worldstate that the goal he visualizes as the paramount attainment needs no more concrete expression than three black chevrons on his sleeve—three black chevrons which are collateral for both his own self-respect and the respect of others. Of material enjoyments one can assuredly obtain enough, and more than enough (and therefore I suspect that the old civilian-capitalistic twelve-room apartments were hardly anything more than a symbol), but of this something, most subtle of all, pursued in the shape of insignia, there can never be a surfeit. No one can enjoy so much esteem, and so much self-esteem, that he does not crave for more. On this, the most sublime, most lofty, and most sought after, rests our solid social system, secure for all time.

These were my thoughts as I stood at the subway exit and saw only as in a dream the guards patrolling along the barbed wire fence surrounding our district. Four trains had arrived, four times the mass of humanity had streamed up into daylight, when at last Linda emerged through the turnstile. I rushed up to meet her and side by side we walked homewards.

To talk was of course out of the question due to the constant maneuvers of the air force which day and night prevented any conversation out of doors. Anyway, she acknowledged my happy looks and nodded encouragingly, although serious as ever. Not until we reached our living-complex and the elevator was taking us underground to our apartment did a comparative quiet envelop us—the noise of the subway which shook the walls was not loud enough to hinder conversation—yet we cautiously delayed all talk until we were inside our home. Had someone happened to overhear us in the elevator no suspicion could have been more natural than that we were discussing subjects which we did not wish the children or the home-assistant to hear. Cases were indeed on record where the State enemies and other criminals had attempted to use the elevator as a place of conspiracy; this was obviously safer since police-ears and police-eyes for technical reasons could not be installed in the elevators, and the janitor of course could not be expected to listen at the elevator opening every moment since he also had other duties. Cautiously, then, we said nothing until we reached our family room, where the home-assistant for that week had already put the evening meal on the table and was waiting with the children, whom she had fetched from the apartment house kindergarten. She seemed a decent and capable sort of girl, and our friendly greeting was motivated by more than just our awareness that, like all home-assistants, she was charged with the duty to report on the family at the end of the week; this was a reform generally considered to have improved the atmosphere in many homes. There was an air of happiness and coziness at our table, especially as our oldest son, Ossu, was with us. He had come for a visit from the children's camp, since this was home-evening.

"I've something nice to tell you," I said to Linda over the potato soup. "My experiment has reached the stage where I am to be allowed to use human material beginning tomorrow, under the supervision of a control-chief."

"Do you know who he is?" asked Linda.

Outwardly it was not noticeable, I am sure, but inside I winced at her words. They might be said quite innocently. What could be more natural than that a wife should ask her husband who his control-chief would be! On the control-chief's hypercritical or understanding attitude, the length of the testing period was indeed dependent. It had even happened that covetous control-chiefs had made their subordinates' discoveries their own, and there was of course slim chance of defending oneself against anything like that. So it was not strange that one's nearest should ask who he would be.

But I was conscious of an undertone in her voice. My nearest chief, and probably also my control-chief-to-be, was Edo Rissen. And Edo Rissen had formerly held a position in the factory where Linda worked. I knew that they had had a great deal to do with each other, and from certain small signs I deduced he had made an impression on my wife.

With her question my jealousy was aroused. How intimate was the relationship between her and Rissen? In a big factory it could often happen that two people would be out of view of others, in the warehouses for example, where bales and boxes prevented a clear vision through the glass walls, and where perhaps no one else might be occupied at the time. . . . Linda also had done her night-guard duty in the factory; Rissen might very well have done his duty at the same time. Anything was possible, even the worst of all: that she was in love with him still, and not with me.

In those days I seldom wondered about myself, what I thought or felt or what others thought or felt, unless it had a direct practical meaning to me. Only later, during my lonely time as a prisoner, have certain moments returned as riddles and forced me to wonder, solve, and solve again. Now, so long afterwards, I know that when I then so eagerly hoped for certainty concerning Linda and Rissen, I did not wish to have assurance that nothing went on between them. Actually, I wished to be assured that she had an outside interest. I wanted an assurance that would put an end to my marriage.

But in those days I would have repelled such a thought with disdain. Linda played too important a role in my life, I would have said. And it was true; no subsequent brooding or intimations about it have been able to change *that*. In importance she could easily have competed with my career. Against my will she held me in a quite irrational way.

One might speak of "love" as an obsolete, romantic concept, but I am afraid it exists anyway, and from its very inception it contains an indescribably painful element. A man is attracted to a woman, a woman to a man, and for every step that they move closer together each one loses something of himself or herself; a series of defeats where victories had been expected. Already in my first marriage—childless and thus not worth continuing—I had had a foretaste. Linda increased it to a nightmare. During our first years of marriage I actually had a nightmare, although I failed to see the connection with her: I was standing in a great darkness with a strong spotlight on me; from out in the darkness I felt the Eyes directed on me, and I wriggled like a worm to escape, while unable to deny my feeling of shame over the disgraceful rags I was wearing. Only later did I realize that it was an expression of my relationship with Linda, in which I felt myself frighteningly transparent, although I did all I could to withdraw and hide myself, while she seemed to remain the same riddle—fascinating, strong, almost superhuman, but eternally disturbing, because her riddle gave her a hateful superiority. When her mouth drew together in a narrow red line—oh no, it wasn't a smile, either of derision or of joy, rather it was tension, as when a bow is drawn—and her eyes meanwhile would be wide open and unblinking—then the same feeling of anxiety filled me through and through, and all the time she held me and pulled me with the same mercilessness, and yet I suspected she would never reveal herself to me. I suppose it is appropriate to use the word "love" when in the midst of hopelessness two people still cling to each other, as if, in spite of all, a miracle might take place—the agony itself having assumed a value of its own, having become a testimony that at least there is something in common: a hope of something that does not exist.

Round about us we saw parents separate as soon as their children were ready for the youth camps—separate and remarry to produce more children. Ossu, our oldest one, was eight and consequently had been in the children's camp for a whole year. Laila, the youngest, was four and had three more years to be at home. And then? Should we also separate and remarry, with the childish notion that the same expectation would be less hopeless with someone else? All my common sense told me it was a deceitful illusion. One single little irrational hope whispered: No, no—your failure with Linda is due to her desire for Rissen! She belongs to Rissen, not to you! Make sure it is Rissen she is thinking of—then everything is explained, and you can still have hope for a new love with meaning to it!

So strangely entwined was that something that was awakened by Linda's simple question.

"Probably Rissen," I said, and listened eagerly in the silence that followed.

"Is it too much to ask what experiment is in question?" put in the home-assistant.

She had of course a right to ask; in a way she was there to keep track of what happened in the family. And I could not see that anything could be misinterpreted and used against me, or how it might hurt the State if a rumor of my discovery were spread in advance.

"It is something I hope the State will gain a great deal from," I said. "It is something that will make any person disclose his secrets, all those things he previously has kept to himself, either from shame or fear. Are you from this city, Fellow-Soldier Home-Assistant?"

Occasionally one encountered people who had been brought in from other places in times of personnel shortage and who consequently lacked the general education of the chemistry cities' people, except for what they had picked up as grown individuals.

"No," she said, and blushed. "I am from the outside."

Further information about where one came from was strictly forbidden as it might be used for espionage. This explained her blushing.

"Well, then I won't try to explain the chemical formula or its preparation," I said. "Perhaps it's best anyway since the preparation under no circumstances must fall into private hands. But perhaps you've heard about alcohol in the old days, how it was used to bring on intoxication, and the different effects intoxication produced?"

"Yes," she said, "I know it used to make homes miserable, ruin health, and in the worst cases lead to a trembling of the whole body, with hallucinations of white mice, chickens, and such."

I recognized the words from the most elementary textbooks and smiled to myself; apparently she had not as yet been able to acquire the general education of the chemistry cities.

"Quite right," I said. "It was sometimes like that in the worst cases. But before it reached such a stage it often happened that the intoxicated one blabbed, disclosed secrets, and did reckless things, because his capacity for shame and fear was disturbed. My discovery has the same effect, I believe, though it has not yet been proven. It has this difference, however, that it need not be swallowed but is injected into the bloodstream, and has altogether a different composition. The unpleasant aftereffects you spoke of are also absent; and only very small doses are required. A light headache is all that the experimental person feels afterwards, and it does not happen, as it often did with the alcohol-intoxicated, that one forgets what one has said. You must realize how important a discovery it is; from now on no criminal can deny the truth. Not even our innermost thoughts are our own, as we so long have believed, unjustifiably."

"Unjustifiably?"

"Yes, of course. From thoughts and feelings, words and actions are born. How could these thoughts and feelings then belong to the individual? Doesn't the whole fellow-soldier belong to the State? To whom should his thoughts and feelings belong then, if not to the State? Only, before this it has been impossible to control them; but now the means have been found."

She gave me a quick look but lowered it immediately. Her expression did not change in the slightest, though I had an impression that she turned a little pale.

"You couldn't have anything to be afraid of, Fellow-Soldier," I tried to comfort her. "It's not the purpose to disclose every individual's little likes and dislikes. If my discovery should happen to fall into private hands, well, then I can easily see what chaotic conditions might result! But of course this must never happen. The preparation must serve only our security, the security of all of us, the security of the State."

"I'm not afraid, I've nothing to be afraid of," she replied, quite coldly, and yet I had only meant to be friendly.

The talk drifted to other matters. The children told about what had happened to them in the kindergarten. They had played in the play-bowl—a huge enamelled basin, a yard or more deep, where they not only could explode their play bombs and set fire to forests and house roofs but also, if they filled the bowl with water, could engage in miniature sea battles, using the same explosives for the naval cannons as were used in the play bombs; torpedo boats also were available. Thus the children played their way into a grasp of strategy, it became their second nature, an instinct almost, and at the same time it was entertainment of the first order. There were times when I envied my children their fortune to grow up with such exquisite toys—in my childhood the light explosive had not yet been discovered—and I could not quite understand why they still longed with their whole souls to be seven years of age when they could join the youth camps, where the exercises were more military and where they stayed day and night.

Often it seemed to me that the younger generation was more realistically inclined than in our childhood. On the very evening I am speaking of, I was to receive a new proof of this fact. Since it was family evening, when neither Linda nor I had military or police duty, and Ossu, our eldest, was home for a visit—in this way the intimate family life was taken care of—I had thought out a means to entertain the children. I had bought at the laboratory a very small piece of sodium which I intended to ignite and let float on water with its pale purple flame. We filled a dish with water, turned out the lights, and gathered around my little chemical wonder. I myself had been highly entertained by this phenomenon when I was small and my father performed it for me, but to my children it was a complete fiasco. Ossu, who already was allowed to build fires, shoot a children's gun, and throw little imitation hand grenades—well, his failure to appreciate the pale flame might have been quite natural. But that not even Laila, the four-year-old, was interested in an explosion which failed to kill any enemies, this startled me. The only one entertained was Maryl, the girl in between. She sat quiet and dreaming as usual, following the spluttering will-o'-the-wisp with wide-open eyes, so much resembling those of her mother. Yet, at the same time as her interest gave me a certain satisfaction, it disturbed me also. Clearly and unmistakably, it dawned on me, Ossu and Laila were the children of the new age. Their approach was matter-of-fact and right, while my own was a remnant of obsolete romanticism. And in spite of the satisfaction she gave me, I suddenly found myself wishing Maryl were more like the others. It promised no good that she thus fell outside the healthy development of her generation.

The evening passed, and it was soon time for Ossu to return to the children's camp. If he had any desire to stay home, or was afraid of the long ride in the subway, he showed no sign of it. With his eight years he was already a well-disciplined fellow-soldier. I, on the other hand, felt a warm wave of longing back to those days when all three of them crept into their small beds. A son is after all a son, I thought, and he is closer to his father than the daughters. Yet I dared not think of the day when Maryl also, and then Laila, would be gone, and only return twice a week for an evening visit. I was very careful not to let anyone notice my weakness; my children need not one day complain about a poor example, and our home-assistant would have no slackness on the father's side to report, and Linda—Linda least of all! I did not wish to be despised by anyone, but least of all by Linda who herself never was weak.

And so the wall-beds in the family room were let down and made up for the little girls, and Linda tucked them in.

The home-assistant had just placed dinner remnants and chinaware in the dumb-waiter and was preparing for departure, when she happened to think of something:

"There was a letter for you, my Chief," she said. "I put it in the parental room."

Somewhat surprised Linda and I looked at the letter, an official document. Had I been the home-assistant's police chief I would certainly have reprimanded her for this. Whether she actually had forgotten the whole matter or purposely failed to investigate, it was considered equally careless not to ascertain the contents of an official letter— it was her right and duty. At the same time a suspicion filled me that the contents of the letter might be such that I ought to be thankful she had been careless.

The letter was from the Propaganda Ministry's Seventh Bureau. And in order to explain the contents I must go back a little in time.

It had happened at a festival two months earlier. One of the youth-camp halls was decorated with banners in the State colors, playlets were presented, speeches given, the participants marched through the hall with drums beating, and all had a meal together. The reason for the festivities was that a group of girls in the youth camp had received orders of transfer, no one knew exactly where; there were rumors about another chemistry city, but there was also talk that perhaps one of the shoe cities might be the destination; anyway some place that happened to be unbalanced with regard to available labor force as well as to the ratio of the sexes. From our city, and probably also from other cities, young girls were consequently ordered to be sent there to re-balance the once established numbers. And now we were celebrating the departure of those called up.

Such festivities always had a certain resemblance to the celebrations for departing soldiers. Actually the difference was great: at festivities like this one, all knew—both the departing ones and those who remained—that not a hair would be touched on the heads of the young people leaving their home city; on the contrary, everything would be done to make them adjust speedily and without complaint to their new surroundings and to make them feel magnificently at home. The only similarity was that all knew, with almost complete certainty, that they would never see each other again. Between the cities only official connection was permitted, carried on by sworn and highly supervised officials, in order to avoid espionage. And even if one or another of the called-up youths should happen to land in the transportation service—an utterly small possibility since such personnel nearly always were trained from childhood for their jobs and educated in special transportation-school cities—they would still have small chance of being assigned for duty on any one of the lines leading to their home cities; moreover, their days off would have to coincide with their passing through. Air-force personnel lived completely apart from their families, and under constant supervision. In short, only a miracle of coincidences would allow the parents ever to see their children again, once they were transferred to another place. Disregarding this—yes, indeed disregarding it since one had no right to linger on such dismal matters on such a day—the festivities were exceedingly joyous, as they should be when celebrating the lasting benefit and welfare of the State.

Had I myself been among the happy participants of this festival, probably events would not have developed the way they did. The expectation of good food (at such times it is always plentiful and well prepared, and the participants usually devour it like hungry wolves), the drums, the speeches, the festive jostling and the cheering in unison—everything brought the hall into great communal ecstasy, as was customary and desirable. I, however, was neither among the parents and other family members nor among the youth leaders. The evening was one of my four each week when I did military or police duty, and I was simply there in my capacity of police secretary. This meant not only that I must remain at my post on one of the four raised corner-platforms and write down what occurred during the evening, together with three other police secretaries in the other three corners; it was also my duty to keep my head clear and make various observations during the evening. If there was a wrangle, if any secret activities took place, for example if any member tried to leave after all the names had been called, it was of great aid to the chairman and the door-guards, who might momentarily be busy elsewhere, if the four police secretaries constantly watched over the hall from their elevated positions. There, then, I sat in my isolation, my eyes scanning the multitude, and even though I would have liked to be one of the participants in the communal celebration, I do believe my sacrifice was well recompensed through the consciousness of my importance and dignity. Moreover, later in the evening I would be relieved by a substitute and could partake of the meal and, at least momentarily, forget my supervisory duties.

There were hardly more than fifty of the young girls saying good-by, and they were easily recognizable in the crowd as they wore gilded crowns, lent them by the city for the occasion. One of them especially caught my idling attention, perhaps because she was uncommonly beautiful, perhaps also because she displayed in her looks and movements a nervous restlessness like a secret fire. Several times I surprised her throwing searching looks towards the boys—this was at the beginning of the festival, while the playlets were being acted and the boys and girls were still separated in their own groups—until at last she seemed to find what she was looking for, when her restlessness transformed itself into a steady glow, as it were. I thought I too could discern the face she had searched for and found; so painfully serious in the midst of all this joy and expectancy, I almost felt sorry for them. As soon as the last act had been played and the youths started to mingle, I saw them cut through the crowd as if it were water and with almost blind assurance meet in the middle of the hall, they alone still, among the jostling, singing humanity. They stood amid the noise as on a silent reef, as if not comprehending the place they were in, nor the time in which they were living.

I started awake, snorting at myself; they had managed to pull me with them into their asocial world, separated from the one great sacrament for all: the communal bond. Perhaps I was very tired, since it seemed like resting only to look at them. Compassion they deserved least of all, those two, I thought to myself. After all, what can be better for a fellow-soldier's character development than early to get accustomed to great sacrifices for great goals? How many are there not, who, all their lives, long for a sacrifice great enough? Envy was perhaps the only thing I could waste on them, and envy there must have been in the disapproval of those two I seemed to sense among their comrades—envy, and perhaps also disdain that so much time and energy was wasted on another individual. For my part, however, I was unable to look at them with disdain; they acted the eternal drama, beautiful in its tragic inexorability. Indeed, I must have been tired since my interest all the time centered about the few .expressions of seriousness which the gay festival offered. Only a few minutes after I had lost sight of the young couple, who were separated by impatient comrades, my attention was drawn to a thin, middle-aged woman, probably a mother of one of the girls to be transferred. She too seemed in some way dissociated from the jostling collectivity. I don't really know how I comprehended this—I would never have been able to prove it—since she participated all the while, moving in step with the marchers, nodding with the speakers, shouting with the shouters. But it seemed to me this happened mechanically, that she was not moved with the collectivity's liberating wave but in some way stood outside, even outside her own voice and motions, apart in the same way as the two lovers. People around her must have had the same feeling; they tried to get at her from various directions. Several times I could see, from my elevated position, how some-one pulled her by the arm, or nodded and spoke to her, but soon withdrew in disappointment, even though her replies and smiles seemed to function faultlessly. Only one ugly, animated little man refused to give up so easily. After she had displayed her tired smiles to him and resumed her still more tired seriousness, he remained, unseen by her, still watching her with definite interest.

This weary and isolated woman seemed in some way to come close to me, without my knowing why. Rationally I understood that if the young couple deserved my envy, she had it to a still higher degree; her self-sacrificing courage was greater than theirs, and with it also her strength and distinction. The feelings of the young ones would, in spite of all, soon pale away to be supplanted by some new flame, and if they might attempt to retain the memory it would soon cease to smart and turn only sweet and beautiful, something of value in life's monotony. The mother's sacrifice could be such that it was renewed every day. I myself was experiencing such a loss, difficult enough although I felt sure I would conquer it in time; I mean the loss of Ossu, my eldest one, and yet he came home for a visit twice a week; and moreover, I hoped I might keep him in Chemistry City No. 4 even after he was grown. Of course I felt that this was too selfish an attitude, towards the small fellow-soldier I had contributed to the State, and I would never have dared show my feeling openly, but in secret it spread a certain luster over my life, perhaps not less because it was so secret and so well controlled. It must have been the same pain with its quality of value that I recognized in the woman, even the same silent self-control. I could not help imagining myself in her place: how she would never again be allowed to see her daughter, possibly never again hear from her, since the postal authorities weeded out private letters ever more greedily, so that by now only really important messages, short and to the point and with the necessary verifications, were permitted to reach the addressee. And then a somewhat presumptuous and individualistic-romantic thought struck me, about some sort of "compensation" that should be given our fellow-soldiers for sacrificing their sentimental existence to the State; and, I thought, it should consist of the highest and best that man might strive for: honor. Since honor was comfort enough, and more than enough, for maimed soldiers in the field, why should it not be enough also for every fellow-soldier who felt maimed inwardly? It was a confused and romantic thought, and later in the evening it was to cause a rash act.

Finally the time came for me to be relieved from duty, and leaving my post to another police secretary, I joined the crowd and tried to melt into the general enthusiasm. Perhaps I was too tired and too hungry for this to succeed. Fortunately, just then the laden tables were rolled in from the kitchen regions, and everyone picked up camp chairs and gathered around the sumptuous fare. If it was by pure chance, or if she purposely had sought me out, I don't know, but strange as it may seem, the very woman I had observed happened to sit down across the table from me. It is not impossible that she had noticed me and read sympathy in my face. Something, however, which did not happen by chance, was that the animated, ugly little man, who had also previously watched her, rushed up and sat down beside her.

To judge from his behavior, he must have decided he was going to force from the woman the secret she wished to hide. Everything he said was innocent enough in itself, but all the time he touched on the wound he suspected in his table companion. He spoke compassionately about the loneliness awaiting the young girls. To avoid harmful group formations, he volunteered, transferred youngsters were as a rule separated from their old friends. There were also the difficulties with a different climate, and the new ways of life they must accustom themselves to. Concerning the shoe cities, which some people were guessing about—and by the way, how could such a rumor get started, their destination was and must remain secret, and the guesses could just as well be false as true!— concerning the shoe cities, it was true that some of them were located as far south as Chemistry City No. 4, but most of them were far up in the north, with its severe climate and long, hard, dark winters, which might cause melancholy in any newcomer. But the most difficult, no doubt, was the language. The common, official language within the vast Worldstate had, unfortunately, not as yet become the universal conversational language. In many places dialects were still in use, entirely unlike each other. He himself had heard, quite confidentially, that one of the shoe cities was supposed to have a very difficult language, completely unlike the one here in construction and usage. But better not pay any attention to rumormongers, the one who told him might not even ever have been outside Chemistry City No. 4!

For a moment I had a feeling that perhaps the little man's behavior was caused by some kind of revenge-desire, but I soon had to give up this idea; from the woman's courteous and minimizing answers I realized they only recently had met, perhaps only this evening. And presently I suspected how things were: the man had no personal reason whatsoever for what he said; all his mercilessness was dictated by the purest concern for the State's welfare. He had no other goal in sight than to unmask this woman who harbored personal sentimental and asocial feelings, make her disclose herself in an outburst of tears, or in a hasty answer, so that he later could point at her and say: See what we still have among us and must tolerate! From that point of view the man's pursuit became not only understandable but even estimable, and the repartee between him and his victim assumed a new significance, as an affair of principle. I listened with great attention, and when at the end my sympathies still were on her side, I felt this was not due to a weak compassion but was caused by something I need not feel ashamed of before anyone: admiration for her almost manly superiority in parrying his thrusts. Not the slightest muscular move in her face altered her polite smile, not a tremble in her voice disturbed her resolutely composed manner, as she met his clever attacks with one reason for comfort shallower than the previous one. Youth finds it easy to learn, a northern climate is often more healthful, in the Worldstate no one need feel lonely, and why do you regret that she might forget her family? Nothing could be more desirable in a transfer.

I was disappointed when the elegant fencing was interrupted by a rough, redhaired man nearby:

"Stop your sentimental nonsense, Fellow-Soldier, whoever you are! Are you trying to blacken the State's actions on a day like this! Even to one of the mothers! Here if ever is occasion for joy! Not worry and sighs."

Just then the speeches were to begin again, and suddenly I had an unfortunate brainstorm: a desire to direct a thrust against the little man. For my evening's duties were not yet over; I was to be one of the official speakers. And so it happened that my speech, well prepared in advance, with gestures and all, assumed a fateful improvised ending:

"... and, Fellow-Soldiers, their heroic deed is not diminished if it is, at times, accompanied by pain. The warrior feels pain from his wounds, the soldier's widow feels pain under her veil, even if her joy in serving the State outweighs this pain manifoldly. Why should pain, then, be begrudged those who must part in their life of labor, in most cases forever. And if it calls for our tribute when mother and daughter, comrade and comrade, part with joy in their eyes and hurrahs on their lips, no less does it call for our admiration if behind the joy and jubilation a sorrow huddles, a controlled, suppressed sorrow; perhaps rather is this *more* worthy of our admiration, more, because it is a greater sacrifice to the State."

Exhilarated and approving as the crowd already was before, it now dissolved in a burst of applause and bravos. But I noticed that here and there among the noise-makers sat those who scornfully refused to clap. Perhaps one thousand applaud, and two sit quietly and refuse, and so those two are more important than the thousand; obviously, since those two might be two informers, while not one of the cheering crowd lifts a finger in defense, once the speaker has been reported—and how could they possibly? It is easy to understand, then, that the situation was not pleasant: I was pathetically moved yet all the time feeling the ugly little man's eyes like a series of arrows. Almost inadvertently I glanced in his direction. Of course he did not applaud.

What I now held in my hand was that evening's aftermath. Who had reported me was not easy to say, it need not have been just the little man. Anyway, reported apparently I was. The letter read:

Fellow-Soldier Leo Kall, Chemistry City No. 4:

The Propaganda Ministry's Seventh Bureau, having considered the contents of your speech at the Youth Camps' Farewell Festival for transferred workers on

April 19 of this year, has decided to advise you as follows:

Since a wholehearted fighter always is more effective than a splintered one, so also must a happy fellow-soldier who never admits, either to himself or to others, that he makes a sacrifice, be granted greater value than a depressed one who is burdened by his so-called sacrifice, even if he hides his depression; consequently, we see no reason to commend fellow-soldiers who attempt to hide their splintering, dissatisfaction, and personal sentimentality under a controlled mask of happiness; only those who, happy through and through, have nothing to hide; consequently, the disclosure of the former is a commendable action for the State's welfare.

We expect you, at your earliest opportunity, to offer your apology to the same gathering that listened to your speech, insofar as this is possible, otherwise over the local radio.

THE PROPAGANDA MINISTRY'S SEVENTH BUREAU

My reaction was so strong that later I felt ashamed that Linda had seen it. And why must it arrive today, in the midst of my elation! To be stricken by this blow at the time of my greatest expectation! Beside myself as I was, I said plenty that was not well considered and which I today, in spite of my good memory, have trouble recalling—that I was lost, my career crushed, my future honorless, my great discovery feather-light as compared with this, which would remain on my secret card in all police departments throughout the Worldstate, and so forth. And when Linda tried to comfort me I thought actually at first that this was pure deceit, and that all she was thinking about was how to leave the sinking ship, even though the children still were of home-age.

"Soon everyone will know what State-threatening speeches I'm making," I complained bitterly. "Go ahead and ask for a divorce, please do, even though the children are so small. It's better for them to be fatherless than to live with an individual dangerous to the State."

"Don't exaggerate," said Linda, calmly. (I still remember her very words. It was not her calm, not the motherliness in her tone of voice, which convinced me of her sincerity; it was the heavy, almost indifferent weariness.) "Don't exaggerate. How many prominent fellow-soldiers haven't some time had complaints levelled against them and later exonerated themselves! How many haven't we heard apologize over the radio, every Friday between eight and nine! You must realize it is not complete blamelessness that makes a good fellow-soldier, least of all a faultlessness in questions where state policies are still being formed. Above all, it's the ability to shed your own point of view and accept the right one."

Finally I became more calm and began to realize that she was right. In my distraught condition I promised both her and myself that I would offer my apologies over the radio at the first opportunity. I even started at once to make an outline for my speech.

"Now you exaggerate again," said Linda, who was leaning on my shoulder and read what I was writing. "One mustn't appear too crushed either, and one mustn't be a rubber band that can be stretched any which way— or you'll be suspected of flipping back in some unguarded moment. Listen to me, Leo, you mustn't write this speech until you're more calm."

She was right and I was grateful that she was there. Wise she was, wise and strong. But why did she sound so tired?

"You aren't sick, Linda?" I asked with apprehension.

"Why should I be sick? We had our medical examinations last week. The doctor prescribed a little exposure to fresh air, otherwise I was completely healthy."

I rose and took her in my arms.

"You mustn't die and leave me," I said. "I need you. You must stay with me."

But alongside my worry about being left alone ran a narrow runnel of hope: yes, why not; why mustn't she die? Perhaps that very thing would be the solution of the problem? But I would not acknowledge it. And so I pressed her to me, intensely, in a sort of impotent fury.

We went to bed and turned out the light. My monthly ration of sleeping pills was exhausted long ago.

Even if her soft warmth, and her fragrance, resembling

tea leaves, had not reached me in wave after wave under our common blanket I would that evening have longed for her, for a closer closeness than simple physical contact can give. The years had changed me. In my youth my sexuality was just an appendage, a demanding companion who had to be fed so I could get rid of him and devote myself to other matters; also a proud tool of lust, but not entirely a part of what I seriously called myself. Now it was no longer so. Fragrance and softness and pleasure were no longer the only things I wished for; the goal of my aroused senses was something much more unattainable, it was the real Linda who at certain brief moments was discernible behind the immobile, wide-open eyes, behind the tense, red bow of her mouth, the one I had sensed this evening in her tired speech, in her wise, calm advice. And while my pulse worked febrilely, I turned over on the other side and suppressed a sigh. I told myself that what I hoped for from the cohabitation of man and woman was a mere superstition and nothing else, as much superstition as when the savages of old devoured the hearts of their brave enemies to acquire their courage. There was no magic ritual which could give me the key and possession of the paradise Linda kept from me. And what was the use of anything then!

On the wall hung the police-ear and beside it the police-eye, equally effective in the dark as in light. No one could deny their good motivation: what nests of conspiracy and espionage might the parental rooms turn into otherwise, especially as they also were used for visiting rooms! Later, when I was given an intimate understanding of the family life of several fellow-soldiers, I was forced to see the connection between the police-ear and the police-eye and the unsatisfactory birth curve in the Worldstate. But I do not believe it was because of the presence of these instruments that my blood ran so cold in those days. At least it had never been so earlier. Our Worldstate had least of all an ascetic view of sex; on the contrary, it was necessary and commendable to create new fellow-soldiers, and everything was done to let men and women from early maturity fulfill their duty in that respect. And I too, in the beginning, had had no objection to someone higher up observing that I was a man. Rather, it had been a spur. Our nights had held the glamor of a gala performance, in which the two of us were no more nor less than solemnly devout and conscientious participants in a ritual, viewed by the State in person. But with the passing of time a change had taken place in me. While earlier, even in my most intimate activities, my first concern had been how I was valued by that Power whose eye hung on the wall, gradually that power had become a nuisance, especially in the moments when I most wildly longed for Linda, and for that never attained and never attainable miracle which would make me the master of her innermost enigma. The eye that now was my first concern, was Linda herself. I began to suspect that my love had taken an unduly private turn, and it bothered my conscience. After all, the purpose of marriage was children, and what had that to do with superstitious dreams of keys and kingdoms! Perhaps this dangerous turn in my marriage might be another reason for divorce. And to myself I wondered if other divorces around us might have similar causes. . . .

I decided to go to sleep but was not able to. Instead, the letter from the Propaganda Ministry's Seventh Bureau started to dance about in my head until I no longer knew on which side I wanted to lie.

"A wholehearted fighter is more effective than a splintered one . . ." That is true, of course, it is logical. And what to do with the splintered ones? How will they be forced to wholeheartedness?

An eery discovery: here I lay, worrying over the splintered ones, as if I myself were one of them. So far I must not let it go. I did not wish to be splintered; as a fellow-soldier I was absolutely wholehearted, without a drop of deceit or treason. The useless ones must go, even she, the thin, controlled mother at the festival. *Shoot the splintered ones!* would from now on be my motto. And your marriage? asked a nasty little thought. But I replied as it deserved: If it doesn't improve I'll get a divorce. Of course I'll have a divorce. But not until the children are beyond the home-age.

And suddenly a thought struck me with clarity and relief: my own discovery was quite in line with the letter from the Seventh Bureau. Hadn't I myself this very day talked to the home-assistant in the same spirit? I would be believed and forgiven on account of my discovery; indeed I had proven to be reliable, and this must weigh heavier after all than a few idle words at a silly little festival. In spite of everything, I was a good fellow-soldier, and would perhaps become a still better one.

Before I went to sleep I had to smile to myself at a comical and satisfying thought, one of those whimsical fantasies that sometimes pop up just before one goes to sleep: in my imagination I saw the ugly, animated little man from the festival standing with a warning letter in his hand, sweating with fear—the big redheaded fellow had reported him for trying to interfere with the joyous celebration and blacken the State. That must, after all, be much worse . . .

Not that it was my habit to waste time, either after my morning exercises or otherwise, but that morning I hurried especially through my shower, I believe, and donned my work uniform in order to stand ready at attention when the door to my laboratory swung open and the control chief entered.

When at last he arrived it was of course Rissen; exactly as I had anticipated.

If I was disappointed I hoped at least it would not be evident. There had been a faint possibility that it might be someone else, but now it was Rissen. And as he faced me, unimpressive in appearance and almost hesitant, I felt quite sure I did not dislike him because there might be something between him and Linda, but on the contrary disliked the thought of an affair between him and Linda just because it concerned Rissen. Anyone else, but not him. Rissen would hardly put any stumbling blocks on my scientific road—he was too kind for that. But I would rather have had a less considerate and more demanding control chief, one against whom I could have measured my own strength, if at the same time I could have respected him. One could have no respect for Rissen, he was unlike others, he was somehow ridiculous. It is rather difficult to put my finger on what was lacking in Rissen, but if I use the words *out of step* it will give a general idea of the situation. That resolute deportment, that precise and measured speech which alone were natural and right for a mature fellow-soldier, were not in Rissen's line. At times he might appear feverishly excited, his words bubbling over each other; he might even allow himself unintentional and comical gestures, or at other times lapse into long unmotivated pauses, withdrawn in thought, occasionally tossing off a careless word which only the initiated could comprehend. Uncontrolled, almost feral expressions would distort his face, even in the presence of an inferior like me, when something that especially interested him was brought up for discussion. On the one hand I knew that as a scientist he had a brilliant record; on the other hand I could not close my eyes to the fact that, even though he was my chief, there was an anomaly between his worth as a scientist and his worth as a fellow-soldier.

"Well," he began, slowly as if the working hours were for his personal use only, "well, I've received a very detailed report about this business. I do believe I understand what it is all about."

And he started to repeat my report in its essential points.

"My Chief," I interrupted, impatiently, "I have already taken the liberty of ordering five test-persons from the Voluntary Sacrificial Service. They're waiting outside in the hall."

He looked morosely at me with his brooding eyes. I had a feeling he might not even see I was there. He was a peculiar one.

"Well, call them in then," he said, as if he were thinking aloud, not issuing an order.

I pressed the waiting-room buzzer. Immediately a man with his arm in a sling stepped inside, stopped at the door, and reported himself as No. 135 in the Voluntary Sacrificial Service.

Somewhat annoyed I asked if no completely healthy

test-person was available. During my work as assistant at one of the medical laboratories it had happened that my then chief had been sent a woman whose entire glandular system had been destroyed in an earlier experiment, and I remembered very well how this fact had almost ruined his whole investigation. I did not wish to risk anything similar. I was also well aware from the regulations that I had a right to insist on healthy individuals for my test: the practice of sending the same people over and over again turned into a sort of favoritism which denied excellent specimens the opportunity to show their courage, besides depriving them of a little extra compensation. A profession like that of the Voluntary Sacrificial Service was of course in itself more honorable than most, and ought really be considered a compensation in itself, but nevertheless the pay was in the lowest bracket, due to the many extra claims for injury which were part of the profession.

The man jumped to attention and apologized on behalf of his department; there had actually been no one else to send; for the moment a great deal of experimentation was taking place in the poison gas laboratory, and the Voluntary Sacrificial Service had been called out to the last man every day. No. 135 himself felt in perfect physical condition, except for some slight damage from the gas experiments, with complications to his left arm; as a personal apology he wished to add that since it should have healed long ago—not even the chemist who had caused it could say why it hadn't—he considered himself fully recovered, and hoped the small gas-injury would not interfere with my test.

Actually, it could not interfere at all, so I relaxed.

"It isn't your arms we need but your nervous system," I said. "And I can say in advance that the experiment will neither be painful nor leave any after-effects, not even momentary."

No. 135 stood at even stiffer attention, as far as it was possible. When he answered, his voice sounded almost like a fanfare:

"I regret the State does not demand a greater sacrifice —I am ready for all!"

"Of course. I don't doubt it," I replied, solemnly.

I felt convinced he meant what he said. The only thing I might object to was that he too strongly emphasized his courage. A scientist too, in his laboratory, can be courageous, even though as yet he has had no chance to show it, I thought. Still, it might not be too late: what he had said about the febrile activities at the poison gas laboratory was an indication that a new war was brewing. Another sign which I myself had noticed but had been hesitant to mention—to avoid being thought querulous and pessimistic—was that the food in all respects had deteriorated during the last months.

I placed the man in a comfortable chair, especially requisitioned for this experiment, turned up his sleeve, washed his inside elbow, and pushed in the small syringe filled with its pale green fluid. At the same moment No. 135 felt the prick of the needle his face began to relax until it almost looked handsome. I must admit that I felt I was watching a hero there in the chair. Simultaneously the color ebbed a little in his face, a reaction hardly caused by the pale green fluid, since it could not possibly have had time to take effect as yet.

"How does it feel?" I asked, encouragingly, as the contents of the needle diminished. Still following the regulations, I wished to ask the test-person himself as much as possible, to instill in him a feeling of equality and thus in a way elevate him above the feeling of pain.

"Thank you—about the same as usual," replied No. 135, but he spoke with noticeable slowness, as if trying to hide the fact that his lips were trembling.

While waiting for the injection to take effect we studied his card which he had placed on the table. Year of birth, sex, race, type of body, type of temperament, blood type, and so on, peculiarities in the family, sicknesses (quite a few, obviously nearly all caused by experiments). I copied the essential information for my own new, especially prepared card index. The only statement that confused me was his year of birth, but perhaps it was correct; I recalled that ever since my assistantship days I had noticed that all test-persons in the Voluntary Sacrificial Service looked ten years older than they actually were. When I was finished with the card index I turned again to No. 135, who had started to squirm in his chair.

"Well?"

The man laughed childishly in surprise.

"I feel so awfully well. I've never felt so well in my whole life. But I sure was afraid . . ."

The moment had arrived. We listened and observed. I felt my heart beating. Suppose the man would not talk? Suppose he had nothing he kept to himself? Suppose what he said had no significance at all? How could my control chief then be convinced? And how would I feel sure? A theory, if ever so well founded, is and remains a theory until proven. I could be mistaken.

Then something happened for which I was not prepared. This big, rough man started to weep in despair. He sank down in the chair until he hung like a rag over the armrest and emitted long, low, almost rhythmic moans. I cannot describe how painful it was; I didn't know how to react, either physically or mentally. Rissen's behavior, I must admit, was perfect; if he was as unpleasantly moved as I, he hid it much better.

This continued for several minutes. I felt ashamed before my chief, as if I were responsible for exposing him to a scene like this. Yet, I could not possibly know in advance what the test-persons might display, and neither I nor anyone else in our laboratory had any special jurisdiction over them; they were sent from a central office in the laboratory complex, where they could be available for all surrounding institutions.

At last he quieted down. His sobs died and he straightened up to a somewhat more respectable position in the chair. Anxious to finish the painful episode I hurled at him the first question that came to mind:

"What's the matter?"

He looked up at us; we felt sure he was conscious of our presence and questions, even though perhaps he did not fully realize who we were. When he replied, it was obvious he addressed himself to us, but not in a manner one uses to one's chiefs, rather the way one might address imaginary listeners or persons of no importance.

"I'm so unhappy," he said, listlessly. "I don't know what to do. I don't know how I can manage."

"Manage what?" I asked.

"This thing, everything. I'm so afraid. I'm always afraid. Not especially now, but all the time nearly."

"Of the experiments?"

"Yes, of course—of the experiments. This time I don't understand what I am afraid of. Either it hurts or it doesn't much, either one becomes a cripple, or one gets well again, either one dies or lives on—what is that to be afraid of? But I've always been afraid—isn't it silly? Why should I be so afraid?"

His first listlessness had now given way to a seemingly tipsy recklessness.

"Anyway," he said, and tossed his head in a drunken manner, "anyway, one is more afraid of what people might say. 'You're a coward,' they would say, and that's worse than anything. 'You're a coward.' I'm not a coward. I don't want to be a coward. And what would it matter if I were a coward? What would it matter if they said so, when I actually am? But if I should lose my job . . . Well, I would find something else. They can always use me some place. But I'll never let them throw me out—I'll quit. Voluntarily, from the Voluntary Sacrificial Service. Voluntarily, as I came."

He darkened again, not over his misfortunes but rather in subdued bitterness.

"I hate them!" he continued, with unexpected intensity. "I hate them, strolling in their laboratories without defect or blemish, never having to fear wounds or pain; or possible or unexpected consequences. Then they stroll home to wife and children. How could one like me have a family? I tried to get married once, but no use; you must understand it was impossible. One is too occupied with oneself in this kind of work. No woman could stand that. I hate all women; they tease me, egg me on, but then they can't stand the sight of me. They're false. I hate every one of them—except my comrades in the Service of course; the women in the Sacrificial Service are not real women any more, they're nothing to hate. We in that group don't live like others. We're called fellow-soldiers, we too, but how are things with us? We live at the Home . . . we are nothing but wrecks . . ."

His voice sank to a blurred mumble, as he repeated: "I hate . . ."

"My Chief," I said, "is it your desire that I give him one more injection?"

I hoped he would say no, because the man was highly repulsive to me. But Rissen nodded and I could only obey. While I slowly injected some more pale green fluid into the bloodstream of No. 135, I said to him, sharply,

"You yourself have quite rightly pointed out that it is called the *Voluntary* Sacrificial Service. What have you, then, to complain about? It is disgusting to hear a grown man complain over his own actions. You must once, like all the others, without compulsion, have volunteered for this work."

I am afraid my words were not exactly directed to the drugged man, who in his half-dazed condition must be somewhat indifferent to reason; rather, I spoke to Rissen, so that at least he would know where I stood.

"Of course I volunteered," mumbled No. 135, dazed and confused. "Of course I volunteered—but how could I know what it would be like. I knew it meant suffering—but of another, more sublime sort—and death—but quickly and in rapture. Not day and night, inch by inch. I think it would be wonderful to die, to flail my arms, rattle my throat. I watched someone die at the Home once—he beat the air with his arms, and his throat rattled. It was horrible. But not only horrible. One can't imitate it. But ever since then I have thought it would be wonderful to act that way, once. One has to, one can't stop it. If it were willful it would be indecent. But it's not voluntary. For once no one is allowed to stop it. One only acts that way once; when one dies one can act any way one wants, without anybody stopping it."

I stood there, fingering a glass stirring-rod.

"The man must be perverse in some way," I said, aside to Rissen. "This is not the way a healthy fellow-soldier reacts."

Rissen did not reply.

I turned to the test-person and started to reprimand him, angrily: "Can you actually be so shameless as to put the blame . . ." I noticed Rissen gave me a long glance, both cold and amused, and I felt myself blush to realize he must be thinking I was putting on airs for his sake. (An extremely unjust thought, I felt.) Anyway, I must finish my sentence, and I continued in a much milder voice: ". . . on others because you have chosen a work which you consider unsuitable for you?"

No. 135 did not seem to react at all to tone or modulation, only to the question itself.

"Others?" he said. "I myself? But I don't want it. It's true of course, I did want to. We were ten in my camp who volunteered, more than from any other youth camp. It was like a hurricane through our camp—I've often wondered why. Everything seemed to point to the Voluntary Sacrificial Service. Speeches, films, talks: Voluntary Sacrificial Service! And during the first years I still had the feeling it was worth it! You see, we went and volunteered; when you looked at the man beside you he didn't seem a human being any more. His face, you see—like fire! Not like flesh and blood. Holy, godlike. The first years I thought: We've been granted something different, and more than ordinary mortals; now we are paying for it, and we can, after what we have experienced. . . . But we can't. I can't. I can't hang on to that memory any longer, it fades, recedes further and further. Before, it would sometimes pop up when I didn't look for it at all, but every time I do look for it—and I must try to see a meaning in life again—it doesn't appear any more, it has receded too far back. I think I must have worn it out by looking for it too much. Sometimes I lie awake and wonder how it would have been if I had had a normal life—would I then have experienced that moment of exaltation once more perhaps; or perhaps not until now—or if all that greatness could have been spread over a lifetime and given it meaning—in any case, then perhaps it wouldn't seem so hopelessly over and done with. One needs a present, you see, not only the memory of a past moment, to live on for the rest of one's life. This way is unbearable, even though one once might have been prepared for anything. . . . But one feels ashamed—ashamed to betray the only moment in life that had any value. Betray. Why betray? All I want is an ordinary life to discover its meaning again. I took too much upon myself. I'm not strong enough. Tomorrow I'll report I'm through."

A sort of relaxation followed. Then he broke the silence again:

"Do you think one might have such a moment once more—when one dies? I have thought of that; I would so like to die. If I get nothing else out of life, at least I'll get that. When one says: I'm unable, one means: I'm unable to live, not unable to die; for that, one is able; die one is always able to, for then one is allowed to be as one wants . . ."

He stopped and sat silent, resting against the back of the chair. A greenish pallor had started to spread across his face. Almost imperceptible fits of hiccup made his body tremble. The hands groped along the armrests and the whole body seemed to come awake with apprehension and nausea. Not surprising, since he had been given a double dose. I handed him a glass of water with a tranquilizer in it.

"He'll be all right in a moment," I said. "It's only when the effect wears off that he feels a little uncomfortable. Then all is over. In one way, perhaps, the most unpleasant task is ahead of him: to creep into his feeling of fear and shame again. Look, my Chief! I think it might be well worth while to observe him!"

Actually Rissen's eyes were glued on No. 135 with an expression as if he, and not the test-person, were feeling ashamed. The man before us was offering anything but a stimulating sight; the veins at his temples strained and swelled, the muscles at the corners of his mouth trembled in suppressed fright of a far more serious sort than the one he had hid when he first entered the room. He kept his eyes closed as with a seizure of cramp, perhaps hoping as long as possible that his clear remembrance might only be an evil dream.

"Does he remember all that has taken place?" asked Rissen, in a low voice.

"All, I'm afraid. In fact, I don't know if this is to be considered good or bad."

With utmost reluctance the test-person at last decided to open his eyes wide enough to enable him to shuffle along across the floor. Bent and shaky he attempted a few steps away from the chair, without daring to look either one of us in the face.

"Thank you so much for your services," I said, and sat down at the table. (Custom required that the one spoken to should reply: "I've only done my duty"; but not even such an inveterate formalist as I was in those days had the nerve to insist on formalities from a test-person after an experiment.) "I'll write out my report now, then you can pick up your pay from the cashier at your convenience. I will indicate Class 8—moderate inconvenience without consequences. The pain and the nausea are really nothing to mention; I should actually have written Class 3, but I feel—well, I don't know how to say it—that you are a little ashamed."

Absent-mindedly he picked up the paper and shuffled on toward the door. There he stopped irresolutely a few seconds, turned suddenly to stiff attention and stammered, "I only wish to state, I do not know what happened to me. I lost my senses and said things I do not mean at all. No one can love his job more than I do, and naturally I have no intention of quitting. I hope in all sincerity that I may have the opportunity to show my good inclinations by suffering the most difficult experiments for the State."

"Well, stay in the Service at least till your hand has healed," I said, lightly. "If not, you'll find it difficult to get accepted in any other work. By the way, what else have you learned? As far as I know, no useless extra training is wasted on a fellow-soldier, and a man of your years can't easily be used in another field, especially as there is no 'invalidism' in the service you've chosen . . ."

I feel, even now, that I spoke arrogantly and superciliously. The fact was that all of a sudden I experienced a definite antagonism toward my first test-person. I felt that I had plenty of reasons for such an attitude: his cowardice, his selfish irresponsibility which he hid under a mask of courage and self-sacrifice when conscious that his chiefs so desired it. Indeed, the Seventh Bureau's line of reasoning had become my own. When it concerned disguised cowardice I could see myself how ridiculous it was, even if I had not noticed it when it concerned disguised sorrow. On the other hand, what I did not clearly realize was another reason for my antagonism, something I have much later discovered and understood: once more it was envy. That person, inferior as he was in many ways, spoke of a moment of lofty bliss, admittedly gone and almost forgotten, yet it was a moment. . . . His short, ecstatic journey to the youth camp's propaganda office the day he had volunteered for the Sacrificial Service—yes, that I envied him. Would perhaps one single such moment have slaked my insatiable thirst which I tried in vain to quench with Linda? Although I had not thought my ideas through, I had a feeling that this man, though favored by grace, was ungrateful, and this made me hard.

Rissen, on the other hand, acted in a way that surprised me: he walked right up to No. 135, put his hand on his shoulder and said, in a tone of voice so warm that it is almost never used for grown people, least of all for men, but most often by some highly emotional mother speaking to her child, "Don't worry now! You must realize nothing personal will get out from here—it's just as if it had never been said!"

The man gave him a shy look, turned quickly on his heels and disappeared through the door. I could appreciate his embarrassment; had he possessed one ounce of pride, I thought, he would have spit in the face of a chief who allowed himself to be so familiar with an inferior. And I thought further: how can I respect and obey such a chief! The one who fails to inspire fear cannot demand respect either, quite naturally, since respect always means acknowledgment of strength, superiority, power; and strength, superiority, and power are always dangerous.

Rissen and I were now alone and a long silence spread over the room. I did not like Rissen's pauses; they were neither rest nor work.

"I suspect what you are thinking, my Chief," I said at last to get going. "You are thinking that this does not prove anything; I might have given the man instructions in advance. Admittedly, what he said was personally compromising, but not punishable. Is that what you are thinking?"

"No," said Rissen, as if awakening. "No, that is not what I was thinking. It seemed clear enough that he said plenty of what he actually felt but wouldn't have wished to say for anything in the world. There is no question but that he was honest, both in what he confessed and in his shame afterwards."

In my own interest I should have been pleased with Rissen's gullibility, but the fact was that it irritated me because I felt his belief was arrived at too easily. In our Worldstate—where every single one of the fellow-soldiers is imbued from earliest youth with strong self-control—it

44

would certainly not have been impossible that No. 135 had put on a magnificent act; although in this case it happened not to be so. But I held back my critical thoughts and only replied, "Would it be a breach of discipline if I suggest we continue?"

The peculiar man seemed not to notice what I said.

"A remarkable discovery," he commented, thoughtfully. "How did you ever get on to it?"

"I built on earlier discoveries," I replied. "A drug with similar effect has been available for almost five years, but the toxic side-effects have been such that almost every test-person landed in the insane asylum, even after a single experiment. The discoverer used up such a great amount of human material that he was sharply warned, and the experiments were discontinued. Now I have managed to neutralize the toxic side-effects. I must admit, I was quite apprehensive as to how it would work out in practice . . ."

And quickly, almost casually, I added: "I hope my discovery will be named Kallocain, after me."

"Of course, of course," said Rissen, almost indifferently. "Do you yourself suspect how great an importance it might have?"

"Indeed I do. 'Where need is greatest, help is nearest,' as the saying is. You know how false evidence is swamping the courts. Hardly a case is stated without directly opposite depositions, obviously not based on mistakes or carelessness. What has caused this flood of perjury no one knows, but it is a fact."

Rissen, irritatingly, kept drumming his finger tips on the table as he asked, "Is it really so difficult to find out what has caused it? I'll put only one question—you need not answer it unless you wish—but do you consider perjury evil under all circumstances?"

"Of course not," I replied, a little annoyed. "Not if the welfare of the State requires it. But I couldn't say the same about any silly little case."

"Think well," said Rissen, slyly, and lowered his head. "Isn't it to the State's benefit that a criminal be condemned, regardless of whether he is guilty or not of the case at hand? Isn't it to the State's benefit if my useless, harmful, most revolting enemy be condemned, even if he hasn't exactly done something legally punishable? *He* demands consideration, of course, but what right of consideration has the individual . . ."

I was not quite sure what he was driving at, and time was passing. I quickly rang for the next test-person, and while giving her a needle I replied to Rissen, "Anyway, on the contrary it has turned out to be quite a nuisance to the State. But my discovery will solve this problem in a trice. Not only can witnesses be controlled now—indeed, no witnesses will be required, since the criminal will confess, happily and without reservation, after one single little injection. We are both familiar with the shortcomings of the third degree—well, please don't misunderstand me, I don't criticize its use when nothing else has been available —one can't very well feel solidarity with criminals while quite sure one has nothing on one's own conscience . . ."

"You seem to have an unusually solid conscience," said Rissen, dryly. "Or do you only play that you have one? My own experience is rather that no fellow-soldier above forty has a very clear conscience. In one's youth, perhaps, some, but later . . . Perhaps you are not forty yet?"

"No, I'm not," I replied as calmly as I could, and fortunately I was facing toward the new test-person so I need not look Rissen in the eye. I was upset but not primarily because of his insolence toward me; what irritated me in still higher degree was his general statement. What an unendurable situation he was picturing—

for all fellow-soldiers who had reached maturity to have a chronically bad conscience! Although he did not directly say so, I felt it vaguely as an attack against the values I considered the holiest of all.

He must have sensed the rejection in my tone of voice and realized he had gone too far; we continued our work without further talk, except that which was professional and necessary.

As I try to recall the next experiments, I find they do not remain with me nearly as clearly or with the same color and life as the first one. It had naturally been the most exciting one, but I still could not be quite sure that my preparation *always* would prove effective, even though it had turned out well the first time. I suppose what disturbed me most was my indignation toward Rissen. However carefully I performed my work, only half my attention was on it, and perhaps this is the reason the subsequent experiments did not sink equally deep into my memory. I will therefore not try to describe all the details; it will be sufficient to relate the general impression.

Before dinner we had processed the five test-persons who had been sent down to us, and two more besides, each one more bandaged and miserable than the last; and I felt completely pulled to pieces and filled with a rising disgust, mixed with fear; was it only the rabble that found its way to the Voluntary Sacrificial Service? I asked myself. Yet I knew it was not so. I knew that highly valuable qualities were required in anyone seeking acceptance; courage was demanded, self-sacrifice, selflessness, decision, before anyone could surrender to such a profession. I neither could nor would believe that the work ruined those who chose it. But the insight I gained into the private lives of the test-persons was depressing.

No. 135 had been a coward and masked his cowardice.

He had at least had his appealing side: keeping the great moment of his life holy. The others were as cowardly as he, some a great deal more so. There were those who only complained, not just about their profession—the wounds, the sicknesses, and the fear which they themselves had chosen—but also about a great many immaterial things, like the beds in the Home, the ever poorer food (then they too had noticed it!), carelessness in the hospitals. One might well imagine that a great moment had existed in their lives also, but in that case it had already sunk too deep to be recaptured. Perhaps they had not used as great will power as No. 135 to keep it alive. The truth was that however poor a hero No. 135 had seemed while under the Kallocain intoxication, when I later compared him with the others he assumed the stature of at least a comparative hero in my estimation. But there was so much else that disgusted and frightened me with the other test-persons we used in those early days: more or less developed abnormalities, eery fantasies, unbridled secret debauchery. We had also a few who did not live at the Home but were married and had their own apartments; they babbled about their marital difficulties in a way that was both pitiful and ridiculous. In short, either one must despair over the Volunteer Sacrificial Service, or over all the fellow-soldiers in the Worldstate, or over the biological species *Homo sapiens* in general.

And to each in turn Rissen solemnly promised that the valuable secrets would be in good keeping. This was difficult for me to take.

After one especially outrageous case—and on the very first day, too, the last one before noon—an old man who fantasied about lust murder although apparently he had never perpetrated one and probably never would have the opportunity to, I could not help giving vent to my painful feelings; I turned to Rissen with a quite unjustified plea in apology for my test-persons.

"Do you really think they are such horrible rotters?" asked Rissen.

"Well, they might not all be potential lust-murderers," I replied, "but they all seem more miserable than is permissible."

I had expected an agreement. It would have eased me a little and removed me as it were from the whole painful situation. When I realized that he did not share my intense disgust, it became doubly painful. But we continued our conversation anyway as we walked to the dining room.

"Permissible, yes, permissible," said Rissen. Then he changed his tone of voice and trend of thought and went on: "You can be glad we haven't encountered saints and heroes of the permissible sort—I suspect I would have felt less convinced then. Nor, I must say, have we come across a real criminal."

"What about this last one, this very last one! I admit he hasn't committed any crime, and I don't suppose he will bring himself to commit any of the misdeeds he fantasies about, old as he is and watched over at the Home. But imagine if he had been young and had opportunities to translate his desires into deeds! In such a case my Kallocain would be invaluable. With its aid one could anticipate and prevent many horrible crimes which now are committed suddenly and without warning . . ."

"Provided one gets hold of the right persons. And that won't be easy. For I don't suppose you have in mind that all people should be examined?"

"Why not? Why not all? I know it's a dream of the future, but still—! I can visualize a time when positions will be filled only after a Kallocain-examination, as they now require psychological tests. In this way not only will the individual's competence be a known fact but also his or her value as a fellow-soldier. I would even go so far as to predict a yearly Kallocain-test for every single fellow-soldier."

"Your plans for the future are not of picayune proportions," interrupted Rissen. "But it would require too great an apparatus."

"You are quite right, my Chief. It would require a whole new department, with hordes of employees who would have to be drained away from established production and military organizations. Before such a change could be effectuated we would obviously have to reach that population increase which we have propagandized for many years but haven't seen any sign of. Perhaps we might hope for a new great war of conquest to make us richer and more productive."

But Rissen shook his head.

"Not at all," he said. "As soon as it was discovered that your plan is the most important of all, the only necessary one, the only one that can quiet our overpowering—yes, our *overpowering*—fear, then you could be sure that the new department would be set up. We might have to lower our standard of living, intensify our work-rhythm, but this great, beautiful feeling of complete security would compensate for what we might lose."

I was not sure whether he was serious or being ironic. On the one hand I would not welcome a further lowering in our standard of living. (One is so ungrateful, I thought; one is so inclined to personal pleasure and selfishness, even when it concerns something so much greater than the individual's own pleasures.) On the other hand I felt complimented at the thought of the importance Kallocain might one day play. But before I had time to reply at all, he added in a different tone, "This much at least is certain —the last vestige of our private lives will then be gone."

"Well, *that* is not too important!" I chuckled. "Collectivity will conquer the last dark corner where asocial tendencies might lurk. As far as I can see it means simply that the great communion is near its fulfillment."

"The communion," he repeated slowly, as if doubting it.

I never had time to answer him; we had reached the dining room door and had to part to go to our places at different tables. We could not stop to finish our conversation, partly because it would have aroused suspicion, partly because we could not halt the stream of humanity longing for dinner. But as I walked to my table and sat down, I wondered at the doubt in his voice and was annoyed.

He was sure to know what I had meant; this was no invention of mine, this about the communion. Every single fellow-soldier, from earliest childhood, had implanted in him the difference between lower and higher life—the lower, uncomplicated and undifferentiated, as for example the one-cell animals and plants; the higher, complicated and endlessly differentiated, for example the human body, with its fine and well-functioning composition. Every fellow-soldier also learned that it was exactly the same with the social systems: the social body had developed from a planless herd to the most highly organized and differentiated of all forms: our present World-state. From individualism to collectivism, from aloneness to communion, such had been the course of this giant and holy organism, in which the individual was only a cell with no other significance than that it served the organism as a whole. Every youth with the child-camps behind him knew this much, and Rissen ought to know it too. Moreover, he should have understood, something not difficult to understand, that Kallocain was a necessary stage in this whole development, since it widened the great communion to encompass also the inner self, which had been kept private before. Did Rissen actually not understand something so logical, or did he not wish to understand?

I glanced towards his table. There he was sitting slouched over his soup, stirring it absent-mindedly. The entire man disturbed me in a vague sort of way. He was peculiar not only in being unlike others to the point of absurdity, he was peculiar also in another direction where I vaguely apprehended danger. As yet I did not know what sort of danger, but my reluctant observation was drawn to all he did and said.

Our experiment would continue after dinner, and now the test concerned a more complicated matter. I had planned it with the expectation of a less gullible control-chief than Rissen, but in any case exactitude was a virtue. My experiments would not remain with the control-chief; if he passed on them they would be discussed in many circles within the chemistry cities, perhaps even in the judiciary department at the Capital. The test-persons we now sent for need not be in good health; it was sufficient if their mental capacities were intact; this we especially emphasized. On the other hand, they must meet a qualification probably seldom required in a test-person: they must be married.

We had contacted the chief of police by telephone to obtain permission for this new experiment. Even though we had full disposition, physically and mentally, over the test-persons from the Voluntary Sacrificial Service, except for considerations of the State's welfare, we did not have unlimited control over their spouses, any more than we controlled other fellow-soldiers. For this we must have a special permission from the chief of police. He was rather reluctant at first, considered it unnecessary as long as voluntary sacrificial individuals were available, and seemed to have great difficulty in understanding what it was all about; however, after we had worked on him long enough to make him impatient—with all his other work piling up—and after we had convinced him that nothing worse would happen to the individuals than the fear and a slight nausea, he finally gave his consent. But he also instructed us to contact him in the evening for a more detailed report when he would be less rushed.

Ten new test-persons from the Voluntary Sacrificial Service were called into our laboratory, all at one time— some men, some women, all married to spouses whose activity was outside the Voluntary Sacrificial Service. In my card index I entered their numbers, and also their names and addresses, which were not included on the personal card, and this action of mine caused a certain apprehension and fear. I tried to quiet them by explaining what we were up to.

The project called for each one of them to return home to his or her spouse and show signs of intense worry; or, if it seemed easier to them, a rosy optimism about the future. When pressed they should at last, in strictest confidence, tell about having engaged in espionage. A neighbor on the subway might have whispered in their ear how to make a lot of money, if they only were willing to draw a map of the laboratories surrounding the Voluntary Sacrificial Service Center, or the relation of the laboratories to the subway lines, or something of that sort. Then they only had to wait and not in any way let on that an experiment was in progress.

The same evening we called on the chief of police, duly provided with a certification from the top chief of our laboratory-complex concerning our visit, as well as a visiting license from the police department, sent us by special messenger. I had managed, with great difficulty, to exchange my evening's military duty for double duty some later evening.

We were quite pleased to have this opportunity to meet the chief of police in person; we needed his help in our present activities. But it turned out to be a difficult task to convince him—not because he was particularly dense, rather the contrary, but because he was in a bad temper, and apparently was suspicious of everyone on principle. I must admit that his suspicion appealed to me more than Rissen's gullibility. Even though, as it happened, he was harder on me, I felt it was as it should be; when finally we had him on our side I at least had the feeling that I had opened a very well secured door with the right and lawful key, not with a crowbar or a kick.

We told him that we needed to get hold of the people in whom our test-persons had confided—that is, their spouses. For all we cared, they could be reported in the regular legal way, as accessories to conspiracies, and taken into custody in accordance with all the rules, as long as they later were turned over to us. If the chief of police wished to let his subordinates in on the secret, or if he preferred to keep the matter to himself, well, that was his business. The only important thing was that persons arrested (non-reporting spouses) must be Kallocain-tested by us. If he wished to check, he could see for himself that the people arrested would suffer no damage from us, and consequently no human material would be destroyed uselessly; he might come in person, or send a representative, we would feel equally complimented either way. Actually, I think it was "come in person" that made him more understanding; in spite of his bad temper he was curious about how my discovery would work. When at last we had obtained written confirmation of his earlier promise over the telephone, with his signature, Vay Karrek, in tall, pointed but strong letters under it, we prepared him for the fact that some of the unsuspecting spouses might be honest enough to report the pretended criminals. Since the whole matter was only an experiment it must of course not lead to prosecution; we handed him a list with the names of the test-persons; we would be most grateful if these people's spouses were apprehended as early as possible on the morrow.

Tired but satisfied with the result of our call we left the police headquarters.

When I entered the parental room after reaching home —Linda had already gone to bed—I noticed a message for me on the bedside table. It concerned my military and police service: instead of four evenings a week it had now been extended to five. For the time being, then, the authorities considered it necessary to limit the family evenings to óne a week, while the festivity-lecture evening remained the same as before. (This last-named evening was of utmost importance not only for the fellow-soldier's recreation and education, but also for the State's continuance. Where and when would fellow-soldiers otherwise meet and fall in love? Linda and I too had those festival evenings to thank for our marriage.) The message was quite in line with the signs I had already observed, and I noticed on Linda's table a similar notification.

All sorts of happenings infringed on the family evenings, this I was already well aware of. If things turned out badly there might be long periods in which I never had an evening to myself. Since it was not especially late and I did not feel as tired as I was after an evening of military duty, I decided to do at once what I must attend to anyway: I sat down and wrote the apology I would ask to deliver over the radio:

"I, Leo Kall, employed at the laboratory for organic poisons and anesthetizing gases, experimental department, Chemistry City No. 4, wish to offer an apology:

"At the youth camp's festival for transferred workers on

April 19, of this year, I committed a serious error. Seized with false compassion, the type that pities the individual, and false heroism, the type that prefers to dwell with the tragic and dark instead of the light and happy in life, I delivered the following speech." Here I would quote my speech, in a lightly ironic tone. of voice. "Now the Propaganda Ministry's Seventh Bureau has criticized this speech: 'When a wholehearted, etc.'" (The pronouncement should also be repeated, since it was the most important part to the listeners, precedented as it was and a warning to all who might be straying along similar lines of thought or feeling.) "Consequently, I wish to take this means to apologize for my regrettable error; I realize deeply and fully how justified is the displeasure of the Propaganda Ministry's Seventh Bureau, and at the same time I offer from the bottom of my heart my unqualified willingness from now on to follow their so overwhelmingly fair view in the matter."

The next morning I asked Linda to look over the apology, and she liked it; there was no exaggeration, no one could discern any hidden irony, nor could it be accused of stupid, false pride. There remained only to retype it, send it in, and then stand in line until it was my turn to speak during the radio apology-hour.

Our experiment took at once a rather ominous turn. Very early in the morning we called the police department to learn if anything had happened, and yet we were apparently too late; in no less than nine out of the ten cases the respective spouses had reported their mates. Whether the tenth one was on the point of doing so, too, was difficult to say, but in any case an order for arrest had been issued, and the person in question would be at our laboratory within two or three hours.

No rosy prospects exactly. I must admit I was a little surprised at how loyal in general and how quick to action these mates had shown themselves to be—most satisfactory, of course, if it had not concerned our experiment. It was evident we must try again; we must at least have a few definite cases to present, before the discovery could be used by the State.

Consequently, we sent for another ten married test-persons, and I repeated my little speech of the previous day. Everything went precisely as before, the only difference was that this time all were in even worse shape; a few came limping on crutches and one had his whole head bandaged up. Granted, that married test-persons are few, and in this particular experiment the crutches meant nothing—but still! Lately the shortage of test-persons had become ever more serious. Obviously, they had been consumed with the passage of time and something must be done if work was to continue as before. As soon as they had left the room, I exclaimed, "But this is scandalous!

Soon we'll be completely out of personnel here! Are we to experiment with dying and crazy people? Isn't it high time for the authorities to start another drive, like the one our first test-person spoke of, to fill up the thinning ranks?"

"Nothing to prevent you from filing a complaint," said Rissen, and shrugged his shoulders.

A thought came to me; obviously—and rightly—the authorities could pay no attention to a complaint from one single fellow-soldier; but one could very well start the circulation of a list for signatures from all the laboratories in the city where test-persons were used and where the shortage was also noticeable. I decided to use the first evening when I was not too tired, if necessary a family evening, to formulate such a petition, which later could be duplicated and sent to the various institutions. Such an endeavor, I thought, could not possibly be anything but highly meritorious.

The hours before the one arrested person arrived were given over to a sort of verbal examination which Rissen conducted, concerning the Kallocain and its closer relations to other drugs, from a chemical as well as a medical point of view. He was an expert in his field, this I could not deny. I think I managed fairly well, and I was rather surprised that he considered me worthy of such an examination. Was it his intention to declare me competent for some higher post? Viewed quite objectively I felt sure I was, and yet . . . It seemed obvious to me that he must have been conscious of my feeling of suspicion and that he should have replied in the same coin. I accepted his friendliness with the strongest reservation. What he hoped or wished from me in the future was impossible to guess. Anyway, I was not going to let myself be lulled into any false security.

As the appointed hour approached, a man in police

uniform entered and announced the chief of police, Karrek, in person. So great, then, must his interest be! Quite obviously it was an honor for the whole institution, and especially for me, that so powerful a man would attend my experiment. With a somewhat ironic attitude— probably he felt that he showed his curiosity too frankly— he sat down on the chair we offered him. A moment later the arrested person was brought in, a fairly young, delicate, and somewhat worn little woman. Either she was by nature unusually light-hued or her paleness was caused by tension.

"You have sent a report to the police?" I asked, to make sure.

"No," she said, in surprise, and turned a shade paler, if that were possible.

"And you don't have anything to confess?" asked Rissen.

"No!" (Now her voice was steady again, devoid of surprise.)

"You are accused of participating in treason. Think well —has no person close to you mentioned any treasonable plots?"

"No!" she said, very definitely.

I sighed in relief. Whether for criminal reason or purely from tardiness, she had failed to report her husband in time; *now* at least she was in no mood to confess; probably she was afraid. Her proud bearing and tight lips would under normal circumstances have indicated a brave and energetic fellow-soldier; now they gave her a refractory and insubordinate look. I almost smiled to myself when I contemplated the artfully planted delusion she was hiding as a valuable secret, and how we would force it from her—we who knew how little it actually was worth. . . . Especially as I thought of all the trouble for nothing she already had experienced, transported in a specially sealed car, at extra speed, on the subway's lowest level, the police and military level, handcuffed and gagged, watched over at all times by two policemen—the usual procedure when a traitor was being transported from one place to another. But my smile had no time to materialize. Even though the story itself was phony and the whole experiment a comedy, her participation in it was real just the same, and equally criminal whether caused intentionally or by tardiness.

When she sat down in the chair she was near fainting. Probably she considered my innocent laboratory a torture chamber where we would now try to force from her what she refused to say. While Rissen revived her I gave her an injection, and all three of us—the chief of police, Rissen, and I—waited in silence.

From this delicate and scared test-person—only an amateur at that, if I may be allowed such an uncritical expression—anyone might have expected a weeping-reaction similar to that of my first victim, No. 135. But it turned out almost the opposite. Her tense features dissolved very slowly into a rapt and childlike purity. The heavy lines on her forehead smoothed out; there flickered across the thin cheeks and protruding cheekbones a surprising, almost happy smile. With one jerk she straightened up in the chair, then opened her eyes wide and inhaled deeply. A long time she sat silent, until at last I began to fear that perhaps my Kallocain might turn out to be undependable after all.

"No, how could there be anything to be afraid of," she said at last, wondering, relieved. "He too must know that. Not pain, not death. Nothing at all. He knows that. Why can't I say it then? Why can't I talk about this also? Yes, he told me; last night he confided in me, and now I realize that he must have known already then what I have found out only now: that there is nothing to fear. To think that he knew this when he confided in me. I will never forget it. That he dared. I would never have dared. It certainly is the pride of my life that he dared, and I'll remain grateful for the rest of my life. I'll live in gratefulness, to do the same in return."

"What was it he dared?" I interrupted, anxious to come to the point.

"He dared confide in me. About something I wouldn't have dared."

"And what did he confide?"

"It doesn't matter. It's of no consequence. Something silly. Somebody wanted information from him, maps and such, and wanted to give him money for it. He hasn't done it yet. He said he thought he might, but that I don't understand. I would never do it. But that he wanted to talk to me about it! I will talk to him some more. Either he will see it my way, or I his; we will reach an understanding and act together when we act. I am with him. With him I have nothing to be afraid of—he was not afraid of me."

"Maps? But don't you realize that all attempts to make maps, of any kind whatsoever, are forbidden, and considered treason?"

"Well, yes, I know that—as I say, I don't understand him," she replied, impatiently. "But we will understand each other. I him and he me. Then we'll act together. Don't you see? I've been afraid of him. And he was not afraid of me. Since he confided this thing to me. Nor has he any reason to be. He will never have any reason. Never. But I realized that it was because . . ."

"Well," I interrupted, with an impatience I would have found hard to explain, "well, then—he had agreed to sell maps to somebody. What sort of maps?"

"Of the laboratories," she replied, indifferently. "But I realized that it was because . . ."

"And you knew it was treason? And that you would be an accessory of treason if you didn't report him?"

"Oh yes, yes, of course. But that other matter was more important. . . ."

"Do you know anything about the man who wanted the maps?"

"I did ask him, but he didn't know very much himself. He was sitting next to him on the subway and said he would show up again, but didn't want to say when or how; only that he would pay when he received the maps. Before that happens we must come to an understanding. . . ."

"This should be quite sufficient now," I said, turned half to the chief of police and half to Rissen. "We have managed to extract all the information her husband was instructed to give her. The rest is of no importance."

"This is highly interesting," said the chief of police. "Highly interesting indeed. Is it actually possible to make people display such openness with such simple means? But you must forgive me if I am of such a skeptical nature. Of course I have implicit confidence in your integrity and ability—of course, without a doubt. Yet, I should like to participate a few times more. Don't misunderstand me, fellow-soldiers. It is only reasonable that the police should be interested in your discovery."

With utmost pleasure we told him he was welcome at any time; we also took the opportunity to hand him the list of the new test-persons. I hoped this group would not be as quick to report as the previous one had been. Hardly was I conscious of my thought before I was struck with fright: did I actually wish that a certain number of people should be treasonous fellow-soldiers? Rissen's words of the day before came back to me: no fellow-soldier over forty has a clear conscience. And at once I was filled with an intense antagonism toward Rissen, as if he had been the one to inspire in me the treasonable wish. In a way perhaps I was right—not that my wish itself was his doing, but without his words I might never have thought of the juxtaposition.

The woman in the chair stirred complainingly, and Rissen handed her the camphor bottle.

Suddenly she jumped up with a shriek. She bowed her head in fright, put her hands to her mouth, and began to cry loudly; she had reached the point when she was fully awake again and now realized what she had said.

The sight was horrible and sad, yet filled me with a certain satisfaction. A moment ago while she sat there, carefree as a child, I had against my will breathed easier; she had radiated a sort of repose that made me think of sleep, although I don't know if I myself show such repose when asleep, much less when awake. She had felt she was secure with another—her husband—and he had already betrayed her, betrayed her from the beginning; and now she too had betrayed him, without intending to. As unreal as his crime had been, so unreal had her security been a moment ago, and so unreal was her fear now. It made me think of the Fata Morgana, the mirage the desert traveler sees above the salt flats: palms, oases, springs; in the worst case he might stoop down and drink from an actual salt pool and perish. So she had done, I thought, and such is always the drink we lap up from asocial, sentimental springs. An illusion, a dangerous illusion.

It struck me that she ought to be told the whole truth, not in order to relieve her of her wild regret, but to make her realize the nothingness of the short security she had harbored.

"Calm yourself," I said. "You have no reason to worry, at least not for your husband's sake. Listen well to what I say now: *Your husband has never met that man on the subway.* He is completely innocent. He has told you that whole story at our instigation. It was an experiment—with you!"

She stared at me and did not seem to comprehend.

"The whole treason-story is a lie," I repeated, and could not suppress a smile, although I hardly felt it was anything to smile about. "Your husband's confidence yesterday was no confidence. He acted on orders."

For a moment it looked as if she might faint again, but then she stiffened and straightened up. As if turned to stone she stood in the middle of the room without taking a step back or forth. I had nothing more to say to her but could not take my eyes away from her. As she now was— closed, stiff, like a dead thing, without a drop left of her blissful security of a few moments ago—she aroused an intense compassion in me. This was a weakness to feel ashamed of but it was too strong for me. I forgot the chief of police, I forgot Rissen, and I was filled with an obscure wish to make her understand that I felt as she did now. . . . From this painful second of trance I was awakened when the chief of police said, "I consider this woman should remain in custody. Admittedly, the treason itself was simulated, but the participation in it was as real as could be. On the other hand, though, we can't exactly pass judgment without the legal formalities."

"Impossible!" exclaimed Rissen in confusion. "This is an experiment, we must think of our personnel, or rather, their mates . . ."

"Why do you want me to take that into consideration?" asked Karrek, laughingly.

For once I was fully on Rissen's side.

"Such an imprisonment would undoubtedly become known," I said, "even if we should dismiss her husband and transfer him elsewhere, which is difficult enough to do—those in the Sacrificial Service usually being in poor health. The story would get out wherever he is placed, a great detriment to the recruiting of this profession; it's already low, it would probably sink to a catastrophic level. I plead with you—everything taken into consideration—forget about this detention!"

"You exaggerate," said Karrek. "The story need not get out at all. And why need her husband be employed elsewhere? He can so easily have an accident on his way home."

"It can't be your intention to remove one of our few and valuable test-persons," I pleaded. "As far as the woman is concerned she is no longer dangerous; another time she won't accept confidences so lightly. And by the way," I added with a sudden thought, "if you arrest our test-person it can only mean that you have made Kallocain a legal means of investigation already, and you yourself said that this was too early, my Chief."

Karrek narrowed his eyes to two small slits, smiled pointedly yet kindly, and said, as if speaking to a child, "Well, well, you do have the gift of speech and logic. For the sake of the laboratory I'll relent about the arrest, although it does not give me personal pleasure. I must leave now"—he looked at his watch—"but I'll be back for more experiments."

He left, and the woman was liberated from her handcuffs. Both on behalf of the laboratory and for her sake I sighed with relief. When she was led out she walked stiffly like a somnambulist, and for the second time a horrible thought rushed through me, caused by this woman: suppose after all I was mistaken, suppose my Kallocain should turn out to have the same dangerous aftereffects as its predecessors, perhaps not for all, but on especially sensitive nervous systems? But I quieted such a thought, and none of my evil apprehensions materialized; through her husband I later learned that she acted in a fully normal way, if perhaps a little more uncommunicative than before. "But closed she has always been," he added.

When we were alone again Rissen said, "There you could see the germ of another kind of communion."

"Communion?" I said, confused. "How do you mean?"

"In her, the woman."

"Oh," I said, still more confused. "But that sort of communion—well, you're right, my Chief, a germ of communion perhaps one could call it, but that's all! That sort of communion existed in the Stone Age! In our time it is a rudiment, and a harmful rudiment at that. Am I not right?"

"Hm," was all he said.

"But isn't this a typical example of where it leads if individuals are too closely bound to each other!" I pleaded my case. "Then the most important tie of all will burst, the tie with the State!"

"Hm," he said again. And a moment later: "It might not have been so bad to live in the Stone Age."

"A matter of taste, of course; if one prefers war of individuals against individuals to the well-organized State, built on mutual aid, then perhaps it was comfortable during the Stone Age. It seems incredible that there are Neanderthal people in our midst."

I had actually meant him but felt frightened after I had said it, so I added, "I mean that woman, of course."

It seemed, to be sure, that he turned away to hide a smile. Most annoying, the way words sometimes slip out, even without Kallocain, I thought.

When I returned home at the end of my workday the janitor told me that someone in the district had asked for a temporary surface-license in order to meet me personally. I looked at the name—Kadidja Kappori. Unfamiliar. At least I could not recall having heard it before. The janitor had not quite understood over the telephone the reason for her call but he thought it concerned some divorce. Utterly mystifying! At last I became so curious that I threw all caution to the wind and signed the paper, indicating I was willing to see her, and when. I made sure that the janitor also signed, that he was aware of the visit and would control the time; then it only remained to forward the petition to the district controller who would issue the license and send it to the applicant.

Then Linda and I hurried through the evening meal and departed to our military service in different directions. These duties had been increased, not only in kind but in degree; during the immediately following days I remember that I considered my work at the laboratory the least demanding part of the day, while my heaviest duty consisted of the evening military service, often extended through the night. I was pleased that my work of discovery was completed; had I been ever so little slower it might never have reached the finished state, in view of the way my evenings were occupied now. With such exhausting hours behind me I would never have been able to gather my thoughts for clear calculation in daytime. Fortunately, only the final application remained and this progressed on its own momentum, especially since Rissen's presence kept me awake. I noticed that he too was very tired, but since he was much older than I, I supposed that his night exercises might not be so severe; anyway, I never caught him in a mistake.

The experiments, however, seemed to have come to a deadlock—the husbands and wives were too quick to report their mates. We had to call in group after group and meanwhile go through the same tests as during the first day.

When we had repeated our attempt for the third time without a single man or woman having waited long enough to report to warrant an arrest—and what a problem it was to get together enough married test-persons (the last time it took us three days!)—finally my free evening of the week arrived, and no pleasure could have tempted me more alluringly than the thought of getting to bed a few hours earlier than usual. The children were already asleep, the home-assistant had left, I had set the alarm-clock and stretched a final time before starting to undress, when the doorbell rang.

Kadidja Kappori! I thought at once, and cursed my compliance in signing that useless petition for a visit. Worst of all, I was alone; Linda had been forced to use her free evening for a meeting of a committee planning a banquet in honor of the retiring chief of food factories in the city and of the woman who was succeeding her.

Opening the door I faced an elderly woman, big, rough, and not too intelligent looking.

"Fellow-Soldier Leo Kall?" she asked. "I am Kadidja Kappori, and you have had the kindness to grant me a call."

"I'm terribly sorry, but I happen to be alone at home and can't receive you," I said. "Too bad—perhaps you've come a long way to keep your appointment, but I'm sure you are familiar with the many instances when the accused has had difficulty in proving his innocence, because there were no witnesses and the police didn't happen to be observing that particular room . . ."

"But this is nothing of that kind," she pleaded. "I assure you I come with the most open intentions."

"Naturally I have no reason to suspect you personally," I said. "But you must admit that anyone can say that. For my own security I feel it's safest not to let you in. I do not know you and no one knows what you might say about me afterwards."

All the time I had been speaking loudly to convince my neighbors of my innocence; perhaps it was this that gave her an idea.

"Couldn't we ask some neighbor to step in as a witness," she suggested. "Even though I must say I would rather have spoken with you alone."

Undeniably a solution. I rang the nearest doorbell; a personnel physician at the Experimental Laboratories' dining rooms lived there. I can't say I knew more about him than what he looked like and that his wife sometimes argued a little too loud for the thin walls of our complex. He opened the door and raised his eyebrows as I told him my errand. Slowly he relaxed, grew interested, and finally agreed. He too was alone at home. For a moment I regretted having disturbed him and wondered if it were wise, but I had no reason to suspect that he was in conspiracy with Kadidja Kappori.

And so both of them stepped into the parental room, as I quickly raised the wall-bed to make more room and make it appear a little more cosy.

"You can't know who I am," she began. "I am married to Togo Bahara of the Voluntary Sacrificial Service."

My heart sank, although I tried to suppress my antagonism; here then was one of our loyal fellow-soldiers who ruined my experiments; probably she had come to report on her husband, although I could not understand why she had come to me instead of the police. Perhaps she suspected something was wrong; or did she consider it less brutal to report him to his chief? Anyway, it was too late to stop her now since I already had let her in and the doctor was sitting there as a witness.

"Something terribly sad has happened at home," she continued, her eyes lowered. "The other day my husband came home and told me something horrible, the most horrible of all—treason. I couldn't believe my ears. For twenty years we've stuck together, put several children into the world, so I thought I knew him all right. Well, he has had his periods of nervous irritation and depression but I guess that's part of the job. I myself, I'm a washerwoman at the Central Laundry of the district, and they give us our apartment. But that's beside the point. But you must realize I thought I knew him. Not that we talk so much to each other—after a few years of marriage you know very well what you have to say, and better leave it unsaid. But you feel what the other wants and means, after living together for twenty years in two rooms. You don't think of him any more than you would of your own hand, but it would be awfully funny if that hand suddenly turned out to be a foot, and started to walk off by itself. . . . And then comes this! First I thought: silly nonsense! Togo *cannot* have done this. Then I said to myself: No one can be sure: haven't we heard that both on the radio and in lectures, and it says so on the placards in the subway and on the streets: NO ONE MUST BE SURE! YOUR CLOSEST RELATION MIGHT BE A TRAITOR! I hadn't thought of this too much before, I didn't feel it had anything to do with me. But what I suffered in one single night I'm unable to tell you. If my hair hadn't been gray already it would certainly have turned that night. It was so impossible to imagine that Togo, my Togo, was a traitor. But what do traitors look like? Don't they look like other people? It's only inside they're different. Otherwise there would be no trick to it. And that they pretend to be like others is only natural, that shows how sly they are. Well, in that way I lay there and made over my Togo. And when I woke in the morning, he was indeed no longer a human being in my eyes. NO ONE MUST BE SURE! YOUR CLOSEST RELATION MIGHT BE A TRAITOR! He was not a human being any more, he was lower than a beast. For a moment I felt it must have been a nightmare—there he was standing shaving in his usual way—and I thought if I could change his mind it might be as before. But then I thought, that's not the way one does with traitors, for they won't change, and only to listen to such a one can be dangerous. Since he was rotten inside. So I called the police as soon as I got to work, it was the only thing I could do, the way he was inside. I thought they would come and pick him up at once, and when he returned as usual in the evening, I waited any moment for the police. He noticed it, and said, 'You've reported me to the police. You shouldn't have. It was only an experiment, and now you've ruined everything.' But tell me now—how could I believe him? How could I believe he was a human being again? When I finally realized it was true—well, I just wanted to hug him in pure joy. But can you imagine it, he got angry! And *wanted to get a divorce.*"

"Well, that was quite remarkable," was all I could say.

She swallowed and swallowed in order not to make a fool of herself by crying.

"You see, I still want him," she continued. "And I think it's unfair he should want a divorce when I haven't done anything wrong."

It was true; she was right; she ought not to be punished for acting like a good and faithful fellow-soldier. She should be compensated. She should be allowed to keep her Togo.

"He feels he can't trust me any longer," she went on, after many swallows. "Of course he can trust me, when he is a human being. And it's equally true that a traitor will find no trust in me, Kadidja Kappori!"

A vision of that other haggard woman's transfixed face arose in my memory with a sad hopelessness. What an immature and meaningless demand it is to wish to possess a single individual, and to trust this person on purely personal grounds, regardless of what he or she does! Yet I had to admit there was a sweet allurement in it. The babe and the Stone Age savage survive, perhaps not only in some, I thought, but in all of us, although to a higher or lesser degree, and that is the essential difference. And in the same way as I had felt it my duty to crush the pale woman's dream, equally strongly did I realize the need of crushing the same illusion in Kadidja Kappori's husband, even if I must sacrifice another free evening for the purpose.

"Come to me, both of you, at one of these hours," I said, and wrote down my free hours on a slip of paper. "If he doesn't change his mind I'll give him something to think about."

She said good-by, expressing much gratitude, and I followed her and the doctor to the door. The doctor seemed to take the whole thing as a joke; he had, annoyingly, smiled most of the time, and he was still chuckling as he disappeared into his own apartment. I could not look at it in that way; I could see the principal implication in the case too clearly to pay any attention to the ridiculous people involved.

I could not help relating the story to Rissen while we

worked together in the laboratory. Actually, it had nothing to do with our work but it had nevertheless a general meaning. I have also a strong suspicion that I was prompted by a certain desire to appear interesting and independent, a man others looked up in time of difficulties, and who would easily and speedily help them set things straight. The fact was that as much as I criticized Rissen, and as deeply as I suspected him, equally important nevertheless was his opinion of me. Every time I discovered myself trying to impress him, I felt ashamed of myself and smothered my weakness. But half an hour later it was there again, and I was doing all I could to earn the respect of this peculiar man, for whom no one could have respect. When I suspected that I failed I tried at least to irritate him, and reasoned that I had a conscious plan with my silly tricks: if I could get him really angry, I would at least know where I had him, I said to myself.

In our conversation I mentioned Kadidja Kappori's words: "He wasn't a human being any longer."

"Human being!" I said. "What a *mystique* people have built up around that word! As if it were something entitled to respect that one is a human being! Human being! It is only a biological concept; if it is something else it should be put an end to, as soon as possible."

Rissen only looked at me with an expression difficult to interpret.

"Take for example this Kadidja Kappori," I continued. "In order to act rightly she must get rid of those repressions, displayed in the superstitious idea that her husband was a 'human being'—within quotation marks—for biologically speaking he could never in all eternity be anything else. She was able to manage that crisis in one night, but how many can do that? A little slower off the mark and she would have found herself among the traitors, without herself knowing how it had happened,

73

precisely for the sake of that superstition. . . . I think it will be necessary to start from the beginning and wean people away from the 'human being'—within quotation marks—in our fellow-soldiers."

"I don't think many are victims to that sort of mysticism," said Rissen, slowly, his eye to a graduated measuring glass he had just filled.

What he said was nothing remarkable, nor anything to remark about, but he had a way of dropping his words in one's ears, as if much were hidden behind. This affected me so that I always wondered what he had said, and his words, voice, and intonation returned and worried me.

Otherwise that very week was so filled with exciting happenings that everything else was forgotten. Indeed, that important week started Kallocain on its triumphal march through the Worldstate. But I shall put off telling about those happenings and instead finish my story about the Bahara-Kappori couple.

They came to see me exactly one week after Kadidja Kappori's first visit. Linda was again out with her banquet committee, but since I now was sure of their intentions and knew I could keep them under control, I did not bother to call in any witnesses. Both looked sullen and depressed, and obviously no reconciliation had as yet taken place.

"Well, well," I said, to help them get started (I considered the best approach was to treat the whole matter lightly), "it looks as if your extra pay was too low this time, Fellow-Soldier Bahara. A divorce can almost be said to be a permanent injury. By the way, that crutch of yours —did you acquire that in your work, or is it—well—shall I say, a result of the marital situation?"

He did not reply, only remained sullen. His wife nudged him. "You must at least answer your chief, Togo dear! Imagine, being married twenty years and then start divorcing because of this! It isn't fair—first to come and fool me with an experiment, and then get mad when I react logically!"

"If you could have me put in prison, you can as well get along without me if I'm innocent," said the husband, grumpily.

"It isn't the same at all!" she interrupted. "If you had been what you tried to make me believe you were, so help me if I had dared keep you in the house! But since you are not—since you actually are the same as I've known for twenty years—then it's clear I wish to keep you! And I've done nothing wrong to deserve you leaving me."

"Please, answer me, Fellow-Soldier Bahara," I said, less jokingly this time. "Do you really consider that your wife did something wrong when she reported you?"

"I don't know if she's done wrong exactly . . ."

"What would you yourself do if someone confided to you that he was a spy? You shouldn't have to doubt about that too long, I hope. Must I tell you what you would do? —Go straight to the nearest postbox or telephone and report him as soon as possible. Am I not right? You would, wouldn't you?"

"Well, of course—but that would hardly be the same thing."

"I'm glad to hear you say you would—otherwise you would be a criminal. Your wife has done exactly the same thing. What do you mean when you say it would hardly be the same thing?"

This was difficult for him to explain. He made a few attempts. "How can she really believe just any old thing about me? After twenty years! And suppose—suppose I one day did something silly, and came to her because I didn't know what in the world to do . . ."

"Then it would be too late to regret it anyway. And as for 'believing' anything, don't you know it is your duty to be suspicious? The State's welfare demands this. Twenty years is a long time, I admit that, but one *can* be mistaken after twenty years. No, you have nothing to complain about."

"No—but if she . . . I wouldn't then . . ."

"Be careful of your tongue, Fellow-Soldier! You might easily destroy my good opinion of your honor. Your wife reported a spy. Was it right or wrong?"

"Well—I suppose perhaps it was right."

"Well and good: it was right. She reported a spy, but that spy was not you. And now you want a divorce because she did the right thing about someone who wasn't you. Is this rhyme and reason?"

"But—well—it feels—I feel unsure when I look at her and don't know what she thinks of me."

"If I were in your place I would be careful not to divorce my wife because she did the right thing. And this apart from the fact that your profession is not particularly appealing to women—nor is your present physical condition, as far as that goes. No decent woman would give you a second look if this story got out; and I would see to it that it came out, and there you would be, with a taint for all time, for all to talk about."

"But I'm uneasy this way," mumbled the husband, more and more confused. "I don't want to have it this way."

"You really surprise me," I said, with increasingly cold tone of voice. "You make me believe you are asocial. This is something we must keep in mind at the laboratory. Would it be pleasant to have such a label attached to you?"

This had effect. His confusion took on an aspect of fear. Helplessly he turned his staring eyes from his wife to me and back again. After a short pause, I resumed, "But I feel sure you don't want to make it as bad as that. You only wanted to make sure that your wife had got rid of her suspicions. She has indeed, that you can see. And then there is no cause for a divorce. Am I right?"

"Ye-es," he admitted, relieved by my friendliness, even though he had been unable to follow my reasoning. Of course, there was no reason, then, for a divorce.

The wife, on the other hand, realizing that the danger was over and everything as before, brightened in intense relief. Her gratefulness had to be my only compensation for two wasted free evenings. Togo Bahara's sullen coldness disturbed me, it is true, but I hoped it would thaw out gradually. To help him get started I called after them, "You come and report to me if your husband really meant what he said, if he actually is asocial!"

Bahara knew I was his chief. Kadidja Kappori's marriage was saved.

That very week our experiment had been unusually successful. No fewer than three in the group of ten failed to make the anticipated report, and fortunately the police had been quick to arrest them. Consequently we had three unsuspecting outsiders at our disposal. Police Chief Karrek appeared in person at the examination. Tall, slim he sank down in the chair, stretched out his long legs, folded his hands across his narrow waist, and waited with an expectant fire in his slits of eyes. The chief of police was a remarkable man, destined from birth to go very far. His bearing could be as slack as Rissen's—even slacker— yet he never appeared unmilitary. While Rissen was supported by his own impulses, seemingly dragged along rather than directing, Karrek's shrunken slouch was only the crouch before the spring, and in his hard, closed face, in the glint behind the half-closed eyelids, lay the warning that it would be a beast's spring, never missing its prey. I not only felt respect for his strength, I also hitched my hopes to his power. In this I soon discovered that I was correct.

The three arrested persons were brought in and examined, one at a time. Two of them belonged to a type we had not previously encountered; common criminal types, simply lured beyond resistance by the sums the spy was said to have promised. One of them, a woman, also entertained both the chief of police and us with intimate disclosures of her husband's nature and habits; an intelligent woman, and sharp, but not a desirable fellow-soldier, and with the most impenetrable individual selfishness.

The third one, however, gave us something to think about.

The reason he had not reported his wife remained obscure, apparently even to himself. On the one hand he expressed an almost ecstatic gratefulness for his wife's confidence—like the little pale woman we had had before; on the other hand, neither did he have any interest in the promised money. Even though he refused to deny entirely the possibility that his wife was a spy, obviously neither was he quite sure that things were exactly as she had said. All in all, perhaps one could say that a certain indolence had prevented him—an indolence he might have overcome within a few days, though it was impossible to say. If Karrek had not decided in advance to temper justice with mercy, that very indolence would in itself have stamped him as treasonous. While such an indolent person gathered his senses for action, the whole treason might already have taken place and the damage been done; but not only that, his whole attitude of doubt bespoke an incredibly feeble devotion to the State. And so it came as no surprise to us when, among other remarks that slipped out, he said, "After all, that sort of business is of so much less importance than *ours*."

I pricked up my ears and I could see the chief of police was doing the same.

"*Your* business?" I asked. "Who are *you?*"

He shook his head with a silly smile.

"Don't ask," he said. "We have no name, no organization. We only are."

"*How* are you? How can you say *we* if you have neither name nor organization? Who are the members?"

"Many, many. But I know only a few. I have seen many but I don't know most of them by name. Why would I need know that? We know that it's *we*."

As he already was showing signs of wakening, I looked questioningly first to Rissen and then to the chief of police.

"By all means, go on," muttered Karrek between his teeth. Rissen also nodded approvingly, and I gave the man another injection.

"Well, let's have it: the names of those you know?"

With perfect accommodation and innocence, without the slightest hesitation, he rattled off five names. Those were the only ones, he insisted; he knew no more. Karrek signaled to Rissen to be sure and write down the names correctly, which he did.

"And what kind of revolution do you have in mind?"

In spite of the injection he did not reply. He writhed under the question and seemed to make an effort, without result. For a moment I thought again that perhaps Kallocain under certain circumstances was without effect, and I already felt drops of cold perspiration. But perhaps the question was poorly formulated, maybe too complicated so that he would have been unable to answer even if awake, although I must say, it seemed simple enough to me.

"You must want something—isn't it so?" I asked, guardedly.

"Yes, yes of course we want something . . ."

"And what is it?"

Again silence. Then with both hesitation and effort, "We want to be . . . we wish to become—something else . . ."

"Well! And what do you wish to become?"

Silence. A deep sigh.

"Any definite positions you wish to obtain?"

"No, no—nothing of that sort."

"You wish to be something else than fellow-soldiers in the Worldstate?"

"N-no. No. Well—no, nothing like that . . ."

I was getting confused. Then Police Chief Karrek, in a soundless motion, pulled up his legs, stooped forward over his folded hands, narrowed his eyes, and said in a low, penetrating voice, "Where have you met those others?"

"In the home of one I don't know."

"Where? And when?"

"District RQ, Wednesday two weeks ago—"

"Many there?"

"Fifteen or twenty."

"That won't be difficult to check," said Karrek, as he turned to Rissen and me. "The janitor ought to know about it."

And he continued with the interrogation: "I presume you had licenses? Did you obtain them under false names?"

"Not a single false name. At least my license was honest."

"So much easier then. Well, go on—what were you discussing?"

But here even Karrek failed; the test-person's replies became confused and vague.

We had to leave the muddleheaded man in peace, especially as the second injection already showed signs of losing its effect. He awoke with a strong nausea. He was not too much bothered in his mind, though—apprehensive but not despairing, surprised more than ashamed.

As soon as he had vanished through the door, the chief of police sprang up to the full length of his elastic height, drew in a deep breath, almost sniffing, and said, "Here is a job! The man did not know anything, I'm sure. His fellow conspirators know more; we'll go from name to name until we reach the brains. It might be a conspiracy of immense proportions, who can tell."

He closed his eyes, an expression of great satisfaction spreading over his tense features. I guessed what he was thinking: This will carry my fame across the whole Worldstate!—But possibly I was guessing wrong; the chief of police and I were of two quite different natures.

"By the way," continued the chief of police slowly, searching first one of us and then the other with his eyes, "by the way—I'll be gone for a short time. Possibly you also will be called away. Be sure to be ready to leave at a moment's notice. The call might reach you at home or at work. To be on the safe side you had better bring along a packed suitcase to the laboratory, a rather small suitcase, with only the essentials, for a couple of days or so. And be sure to have your paraphernalia in order, so you can bring everything along and demonstrate how your Kallocain works."

"What about our military service?" asked Rissen.

"If what I think happens, I will of course make arrangements for everything. If I am unable, well, then nothing will happen. I will promise nothing. And what is your program for the next few days?"

"Continue with more and new experiments."

"Would anything prevent you from following this thread? I mean the last one we interrogated? Instead of using the Voluntary Sacrificial Service we could unravel this mess inch by inch, beginning with the names he gave you; and be sure to record in detail everything you hear. How does that appeal to you?"

Rissen was hesitating.

"In the laboratory regulations there are no directions concerning such a case."

The chief of police burst out in an indescribably sneering loud laughter.

"We mustn't be too bureaucratic," he said. "If you should receive an order from the top laboratory chief—it is Muili, isn't it—I should think you might relax the rules somewhat. I will call on Muili in person. Then all you have to do is to report each and every name to the police department. This might concern the welfare of the whole Worldstate—and you ask for the regulations!"

He left and we looked at each other. I suspect my look was both sure of victory and filled with admiration. In the hands of a man like Karrek one could confidently surrender one's fate. He was made up only of will power; no difficulties existed for him.

But Rissen raised his eyebrows in resignation. "We'll only be a subdepartment of the police department," he said. "Farewell, Science!"

This gave me a jolt; I loved my scientific work, and would miss it greatly if I lost it. But Rissen was a pessimist by nature, I said to myself. For my part, I could only visualize the Staircase before me, and the first and sole question was—did it lead upwards? The rest time would tell.

One hour later, sure enough, an order arrived from the First Laboratory Chief that we were to rearrange our work along the lines indicated by the chief of police. The police department had already been instructed, all we had to do was to pick up the telephone and give the names of the people we wanted arrested, and they would be at our disposal within twenty-four hours.

The first one sent to us was a young man not long out of the youth camp, an amusing mixture of insecurity and proud aggressiveness against a society where he did not as yet feel fully at home. Under the influence of our Kallocain his self-assurance was given a chance to unfold, in a way that seemed rather comical to us grown men, and he entertained us with his far-flung and somewhat obscure plans for the future. At the same time he admitted that he felt most annoyed with the people around him. They wanted to hurt him, he insisted. I had, indeed, suggested that we allow test-persons to speak about themselves as freely as possible, since the previous case had been so difficult at interrogation, but now we were treated to more youth psychology than Karrek could be interested in, so at last I resumed my questioning and asked him if he knew of our previous case.

"Yes, we're fellow workers."

"Have you ever met him outside work?"

"Yes, he invited me to a gathering . . ."

"In district RQ? Two weeks ago last Wednesday?"

The young man started to laugh and seemed at the same time greatly interested. "Yes. What a funny gathering. But I liked them. In some way I really liked them . . ."

"Can you tell us what you remember?"

"Of course. It was terribly funny. I came, and there were only people I didn't know. Well, that wasn't so strange. If you sacrifice one free evening for social life it is usually in order to discuss some subject, something concerning your work, or such, or a planned festival, or a petition to the authorities, and naturally you can't know all present. But it was nothing like that! There were no discussions at all. They were talking about everything under the sun, or sat in silence. That about sitting silent, that made me nervous. And the way they greeted each other! They shook hands! How crazy can you get! That must be terribly unhygienic; besides, it's so intimate I felt embarrassed. To touch someone else's body purposely as they did! They said it was an ancient form of greeting that had been revived, but one didn't have to do it if one didn't want to; no one was forced to anything. But at first I was afraid of them. There's nothing more horrible than to sit in silence. I have a feeling people look right through me; as if naked, or worse than naked. Spiritually naked. Especially when older people are present, for they have had time to learn to look right through, yes, even when they talk—they've learned to talk with the surface and be on guard under the surface. I myself have already learnt to do that, have done it a few times and felt terribly pleased afterwards, as if having escaped some danger. But I couldn't do it with them, they wouldn't have fallen for that. When they spoke they spoke in low voices and it seemed they didn't think of something else meanwhile. I personally like to talk aloud so I can catch the attention of others, I talk aloud and have my thoughts elsewhere. But they were so funny. Finally I got to like it, it was beautiful in some way, very relaxing."

Well, this wasn't much information. The youth must be a novice in the movement, as yet not initiated into the secrets. And to make sure, I asked him, "Did you see if there was a chief for the group? Any insignia?"

"No—not that I could see. Nor did anyone say anything about it."

"What else did they do? Did they talk about anything they had done, or were going to do?"

"Not that I know of. But I had to leave early, I and two comrades who hadn't been there before either, I believe. I don't know what they did after we left. But someone said at the door: 'When we meet out in the world we'll recognize each other.' I can't explain what it meant but it was quite inspiring, and I felt I would actually recognize them—not necessarily the ones I had met there, but any- one who belonged to *them*. There was something especial about them, I can't describe it. When I entered this room here, I knew for sure that you didn't belong"—he nodded to me—"but *you*"—he gave Rissen a dazed look—"I'm not quite sure about you. Perhaps you belong, perhaps not. I only know that I felt more at ease in their company than with other people. I didn't have that clear feeling that they were out to harm me."

I looked sharply at Rissen. He looked so surprised it seemed to me he must be innocent, if by innocence I meant that he never participated in any secret meetings of the sort the young man described. Yet, there was something in the insinuation; in Rissen also there was that asocial vein, reminding one of blind moles.

The youth awakened with a contrition far beyond reasonable proportions considering the rather harmless activities he had disclosed. As far as I could judge he did not worry about his account of the gathering, rather the purely personal confessions which we had yawningly interrupted.

"I believe I must take back some," he mumbled, as he swayed awkwardly on the floor. "What I said about being unsure about others—that was stretching the truth. I only wonder what they want from me. Not that I feel they want to harm me. And all I said about what I wanted to be and do—well, that was only pure fantasy, not a grain of truth in it. It was also an exaggeration to say that I felt more at home with those peculiar people. Obviously, I feel more at home with normal people, when I come to think of it."

"We too feel sure of that," said Rissen, kindly. "In the future, I would suggest you stick to those others, the normal ones. We have a strong suspicion that the meeting you happened to attend is treasonable. Apparently, you are rather free from contamination, but watch out! Before you know it they'll have snared you in their nets."

The youth looked duly frightened as he disappeared through the door.

I don't really know what sort of horrible schemes we

expected to uncover as having been forged after the youth and his comrades left the meeting. Some of the arrested ones, we thought, must have remained to the end. Systematically and thoroughly we interrogated the other four on our list and recorded in minutest detail their revelations, but it took a long time before we began to get a clear picture of the secret gang. Time and again we looked at each other and shook our heads. Were they a bunch of insane people we were dealing with? I had never heard such fantastic stories before.

First and foremost we were after the organization itself, the names of the chiefs, its ramifications. But time and again we were told there were no chiefs, no organization. Of course it is usually true in secret conspiracies that the lower-ranking members are denied inner secrets; all they know are the names of two or three other members, as unimportant as they themselves. We deduced it was this type of members we had caught. We felt, however, that someone would divulge a name of a higher member who knew more. All we could do was to continue.

What had happened after the novices had left the gathering? This was our immediate question. A woman gave us a surprising description. "A knife is brought out," she said. "One among us gives it to someone else and goes to a bed and pretends to sleep."

"And then?"

"That is all. If anyone else wishes to join, all he has to do is pretend to sleep; he might sit down and lean his head against the bed, if that is more convenient. Or against the table, or any place."

I am afraid an ill-suppressed laugh escaped me; the scene called to mind was too ridiculous: someone sitting seriously with a long table knife (of course it must be a table knife, this would be easiest to filch since all one had to do was to forget to return it after dinner) in an extremely serious company. One person is stretched out on the bed, hands across stomach, trying spasmodically to go to sleep, even attempting to snore. One after another pulls out a pillow and places it close by, leans his head in a more or less uncomfortable position and adds his straw to the stack. Someone slides down on the floor in a half-sitting position, leans against the bed, yawns. Otherwise, deadly silence!

Not even Rissen could suppress a smile.

"And what is the purpose of this?" he asked.

"A symbolic purpose. Through the knife he has surrendered to the other, yet nothing happens to him."

(Nothing happens to him! When the room is full of people, snoring but fully awake, ready to look any moment! Nothing happens when one of the guests—all legally registered with the janitor—holds his hand around a table knife that was not sharp enough to cut the beef stew at dinner and listens to the well-feigned snores . . .)

"And what is the meaning of all that?"

"We wish to call forth a new spirit," said the woman, quite seriously.

Rissen scratched his chin thoughtfully. At State historical lectures I had heard—and Rissen surely also—that prehistoric savages would utter certain incantations and perform certain so-called magic rites to conjure forth imaginary apparitions which they called spirits. And such, then, still took place in our day?

From the same woman we managed to get hold of a few references to an absolute lunatic who seemed to play a singular role as hero within their group. It certainly does not take much to be a hero in some circles.

"Don't you know about Reor?" she asked. "No, he doesn't live now, he lived about fifty years ago, in one of the flour mill towns, I've heard; others say in a textile city.

Imagine, you haven't heard of Reor! I would like to give a talk about Reor sometime. But, of course, only the initiated would understand. When you want to talk about Reor you must turn to the initiated. He wandered about from place to place, for in those days it was different with licenses, and some received him from fear, because they thought the police had sent him, and others chased him away, thinking he was a criminal. But of those who received him, not all realized what he was like. Some only thought he was peculiar, but others felt they were secure and comfortable with him, as a small child with its mother. Some forgot him, others never forgot him, and they told of him to the best of their ability. But only the initiated will understand. He never locked his door. He never cared about witnesses or proof of what he did or said. He did not even protect himself against thieves and murderers, and he was in the end murdered—by a man who thought Reor had a loaf of bread in his knapsack. It was during a famine. But he had none, he had already shared it with some men he met on the road. But the murderer thought he lied and had saved it. And he killed him."

"And yet it is your opinion that he was a great man?" I asked.

"He was a great man. Reor was a great man. He was one of us. There are still those living who saw him."

Rissen looked at me knowingly and shook his head.

"The most amazing logic I've heard in all my life," I said. "'Let's be like him for he was murdered!'—I don't understand one iota of this."

"You spoke of initiations," said Rissen to the woman, ignoring my remark. "How does one get initiated?"

"I don't know. One just gets that way. All of a sudden one is. The others notice it, the ones who already are initiated."

"Then anyone can insist he is initiated? There must be some act, some ceremony—some secrets that are shared?"

"No, nothing of that kind. It's noticeable, as I say. One gets it, you must understand, or one doesn't; some never get it."

"How is it noticeable?"

"Well—it's noticeable in everything . . . that with the knife, and the sleep, and it becomes sacred and clear to one . . . and much else . . ."

We were as wise as before.

Whether the woman alone was crazy or all those people shared in her craziness, it was difficult to say. This much was certain, that the magic ritual with the knife and the pretended sleep had taken place; others confirmed it. However, we never determined whether it took place regularly or was just a chance occurrence. Nor could we establish knowledge of the myth about Reor in all, only some had it. What, then, had all these people in common, besides being each and every one of them quite peculiar?

Another woman had a few more names to give us. Consequently it seemed expedient to press her especially hard for details about the organization. Her replies were as confusing as those of the others.

"Organization?" she said. "We don't want an organization. What is organic needs no organization. You build from without, we build from within. You use yourselves as building stones and fall apart outside and in. We are built up from the inside like a tree, and bridges grow between us that are not of dead materials and dead force. From us life itself issues. In you whatever is lifeless enters."

This seemed to me a stupid play on words, yet it made an impression on me. Perhaps it was the very intensity of her deep voice that made me tremble. Possibly it reminded me of Linda, who also has a deep, intense voice, especially when she is not too tired; and I could not help but imagine how it would have been if it were Linda instead of this unknown woman sitting there offering her inner self in such a pleading, penetrating voice. Anyway, I carried the impression with me for long afterwards, even the individual words I repeated to myself—as I thought, because they sounded beautiful in all their meaninglessness. Much, much later I began to discern a meaning in them. However, they gave me a jolt at that time, offering me a first suspicion as to what they meant by "we," what made them recognize each other, what enabled them to have a circle of initiated without an organization, without external signs, and apparently also without any widely accepted teachings and doctrines.

When she had left I said to Rissen, "Something strikes me—perhaps we misunderstood her talk about a 'spirit.' It might also mean an inner attitude, a conduct of life. Or is that too subtle an interpretation for that group of nuts?"

When he looked at me I felt frightened. That he understood me fully, I could see in his face; but also something else; I realized that he too had been impressed by the woman's warm and intense being. I realized that he was even more susceptible than I. And I realized that his very look, his very silence, pulled me in a direction where my whole love of duty, my sense of honor, forbade me to go. In some way he was caught in the snares of those lunatics, and even I had for a moment felt the blissful, overpowering attraction.

Had not the first youth this morning said that Rissen might well belong—to the lunatics, to the secret sect? Had not I myself always felt that Rissen harbored a threat and a danger? From this moment I knew that deep down we were enemies.

We had only one case left, an old man, rather intelligent looking, and at the same time I was afraid of him: no one could know if he also might have the same suggestive strength as the woman. I also expected great things from him; he if anyone should have knowledge about the innermost circles, and if we were fortunate we might find so great proofs that this whole lunatic sect would be condemned and dispatched, a great relief and delivery for me and many others. But he had barely sat down in the chair, when the telephone rang, and both Rissen and I were called to Muili, the First Chief of the Laboratories.

Muili's office was not within our laboratory complex but we need not ascend to the surface in order to reach it: a tunnel three stories down connected directly with the head office, where we presented our identification cards to a secretary who telephoned ahead to make sure we were expected. Within twenty-five minutes we stood facing Muili, a very thin man, iron-gray and gaunt. He barely looked at us; his voice was low, as if only with effort he could manage to speak, yet every intonation carried absolute authority. That man was not accustomed to listening to anyone, except for answers to possible questions.

"Fellow-Soldiers Edo Rissen and Leo Kall," he said, "you have been called to another place. You must discontinue your present work. A police escort will wait for you in one hour and take you to your point of departure. Everything has been arranged for your temporary release from military and police duty. Understand?"

"Yes, my Chief!" Rissen and I replied, simultaneously.

We returned in silence to our laboratory, to put things in order, shower, and put on our spare-time uniforms. Each of us already had a small suitcase prepared for the journey, as well as a box with Kallocain paraphernalia, according to Karrek's order. And at the appointed time we were fetched by two silent policemen and transported via Metro to our destination.

My admiration for Karrek rose further. Fast work,

indeed! Hardly more than a day had elapsed since he left us, and already he had achieved his purpose. The man was a power, and not only in Chemistry City No. 4, it seemed.

When we exited from the subway it turned out our goal was a hangar. A shiver of jubilant adventure filled my being. How far would we be taken? To the Capital? Never having been outside Chemistry City No. 4, I was seized with the wildest expectations.

Together with a group of other passengers we were escorted aboard a well-illuminated plane, the police locked and sealed the door, and from the drone of the motors we soon realized we were airborne. I brought out the latest copy of the *Chemistry Journal* from my suitcase, as did Rissen, but I noticed that he, like myself, often sat back and let his thoughts drift to other fields than the articles and the notices in the magazine. Personally, I tried at least to smother my curiosity when it made itself too apparent. On film I had of course seen yellow fields, green meadows, forests, grazing sheep and cows, even pictures of planes in flight, so actually I had nothing to be curious about, and yet I fought a ridiculous, childish wish that the plane might have the smallest little peephole which I secretly could have peeked through—not that I wished to spy, purely from childish curiosity. But at least I was simultaneously aware of this dangerous tendency. Admittedly, I might never have reached so far in my scientific work had not a certain curiosity forced me into the mysteries of matter. On the other hand, it was a force of good and evil, both, and might lead to danger and crime. I wondered if Rissen had to fight the same inclinations and wishes—if indeed he did fight! Probably he was not one to struggle, he, with his lack of discipline; I had the impression that he was completely without struggle or shame, wishing only that the whole plane were of glass

... A very striking observation, I thought; the man was like that. If I could only use Kallocain for my private pleasure ...

I had dozed off when I felt a light nudge on my elbow; it was the conductor, serving our evening meal—this too had been thought of. I looked at my watch; we had been in the air five hours and must apparently still have some distance to go since supper could not be put off until arrival. My assumption was correct: it took another three hours. If I had known the speed of the plane as well as I knew the time I could easily have figured out the distance from Chemistry City No. 4, and our place of destination, whatever it might be. Fortunately the speed was a closely guarded secret to prevent possible spies from drawing geographical conclusions. The only thing one might deduce was that the speed was very great and the distance, in consequence, great also. Naturally we could draw no conclusions as to the direction; the fact that it was cool, even cold in comparison with Chemistry City No. 4, only meant that we traveled at a great height.

When we finally landed and the motors had been stopped, the door was unsealed by a troop of police who then split up and took charge of the various passengers. (Presumably all were there on important matters, expected and announced; perhaps even, like ourselves, called there.) Rissen and I were escorted to the police-military Metro, where our capsule was propelled with incredible speed to a place called the Police Palace. We suspected we were in the Capital. Through a subterranean gate we were led into an anteroom where we were searched from head to foot and our luggage inspected; then we were shown into some small and plain cabin-like rooms where we were to sleep.

The following morning at breakfast time we were shown the way to one of the dining rooms. We were far from being the only overnight guests in the Police Palace; already some seventy other fellow-soldiers of both sexes, all of mature age, thronged at the tables. Someone was calling to us from his place. It was Karrek himself, who was sitting alone over his corn porridge, surrounded by strangers. Although he was so high above us in rank we felt truly pleased to see his well-known face, and he did not seem to object to our company.

"I have petitioned for an audience with the police president, for all three of us," he said, "and I've reason to believe it will be granted promptly. Be sure to get your Kallocain paraphernalia as soon as you have eaten."

Obviously, I hurried through breakfast and rushed to fetch the box with the Kallocain implements. However, the urgency turned out to be exaggerated; when all three of us had repaired to the police president's office we had to wait more than an hour before the door to the inner room was opened. And since three other persons had arrived before us and were waiting, I expected some more time would elapse.

But we were the first ones to be admitted. A small and agile official opened the door, walked straight up to Karrek, and whispered something in his ear. Karrek pointed to us two, and then all three of us were ushered into another waiting room, where again we were searched from head to foot. Generally speaking the security measures were far more thorough here than at home in our Chemistry City, naturally because the lives to be preserved here were so much more valuable than in other parts of the Worldstate. Even in the first waiting room—and much more so here and in the police president's private room—we encountered guards with raised guns. At last we stood before the mighty one.

A massive figure turned in his chair and raised his bushy eyebrows in a greeting. It was quite apparent that he was pleased to see Karrek. I recognized at once Police Minister Tuareg from our *Fellow-Soldiers' Portrait Album* —his small, black bear-eyes, his determined lower jaw, his full lips—and yet he made a much more imposing impression on me than I had anticipated. Perhaps also the feeling of concentrated Power made me tremble. Tuareg was the brain behind the millions of eyes and ears that saw and heard the most intimate acts of the fellow-soldiers day and night, as well as listened to their most private conversations. His was the will behind the millions of soldiers who constantly protected the State's internal security; this included me when my evenings were devoted to police duty. And yet I trembled, as if this were not my commander-in-chief I faced here, but as if instead I were one of the criminals he hunted down. And I had not done anything wrong! Whence then came this most unfortunate splintering in my nature? The answer was close at hand: all was caused by a suggested false notion, expressed in the words: "No fellow-soldier over forty can have a clear conscience." And it was Rissen who had spoken those words.

"Well, so these are our new allies," said the police minister to Karrek. "Could you be ready to show me a few small sample experiments in two hours? On the third floor a room has been made ready for a laboratory—maybe primitive, but I expect you'll find what you need. If you should wish anything further, only tell the personnel. And we have our own test-persons."

We assured him we were ready and pleased. The audience was over, and we were brought through another door up to the temporary laboratory Tuareg had mentioned. The arrangements here were quite adequate, as long as we were not required to produce Kallocain in greater quantities.

Karrek accompanied us upstairs. He leaned against the corner of the table, in a position so relaxed that in any other person it would have appeared most inexcusable and revolting.

"Well, Fellow-Soldiers," he said, after we had examined the room's work-possibilities, "what have you found out about that secret organization at home in Chemistry City No. 4?"

Since Rissen was my chief it was his right and duty to answer first. And he did, but only after a long silence.

"As far as I can see," he said, "nothing incriminating has come to light. They seem a little unbalanced, all of them, but criminal—no."

"At least so far," he continued after a new pause, "we've not come across a single one with a criminal act, at least not one of sufficient importance in his mind to be divulged under the influence of Kallocain. I make an exception of the man who failed to report his wife for treason, since you must remember, my Chief, that we decided to temper justice with mercy on account of the need for recruits in the Voluntary Sacrificial Service. As far as those people are concerned, I would call them a sect of lunatics, but not a political band. Perhaps not even a sect; they have no organization, no chiefs as far as we have learned, no membership lists, not even a name; consequently they hardly even come under the law against societies outside the State's control."

"You are a great formalist, Fellow-Soldier Rissen," said Karrek, his eyes screwed up ironically. "You use the expressions 'nothing in the regulations' and 'come under the law,' as if printed words were insurmountable obstacles. Is that what you actually mean?"

"Well, laws and regulations are there for our protection," retorted Rissen, morosely.

"For *whose* protection?" attacked Karrek. "In any case not the State's. The State has more use for clear heads who at need can spit on the printed word."

Rissen, reluctantly, kept his silence at this. Then he continued, "In any case, they seem harmless against the State. We can without qualms liberate those already arrested and then leave this whole pack to its fate. From now on the police will be kept busy with murderers, thieves, perjurers ..."

My moment had arrived, I felt; I must make my first serious attack on Rissen.

"My Chief Karrek," I said, slowly and with emphasis. "Permit me to offer objections, even though I am a subordinate. To me this mystical conspiracy appears far from innocent."

"I'm interested to hear your opinion also," said Karrek. "You consider it then a common conspiracy?"

"I won't voice an opinion involving the letter of the law just now," I said. "But I feel that all those people, individually and together, constitute a danger to the State. First I would like to ask one question: Do you consider that our Worldstate needs a completely new principle, a completely changed philosophy of life? Please, do not misunderstand me—I'm fully aware that everyone might need to be awakened to greater consciousness of responsibility, greater effort—but a new attitude toward life, unlike the one we know? Isn't this actually an insult to the Worldstate and the fellow-soldiers of the Worldstate? And such was the very meaning of what one of the arrested persons said: 'We wish to conjure forth a new spirit.' At first we took it as an expression of superstition, in itself bad enough, but this is worse."

"I think you take it too seriously," said Karrek. "My experience has taught me that the more abstract something is the less dangerous are its effects. General expressions can be used, now one way, now another, meaning one thing this moment, something directly opposite in the next perhaps."

"But one's philosophy of life is not something abstract," I said with energy. "On the contrary, I maintain it is the only thing not abstract. And the philosophy of those lunatics is dangerous to the State. This is most clearly seen in their own myths about a certain Reor who seems to have been a cut above the rest of them in his lunacy and in consequence has become their special hero. Indulgence with criminals, carelessness with one's own security (it must be kept in mind that the individual is a valuable and expensive tool!), personal attachments that are stronger than the attachment to the State—that's where they want to lead us! At first sight their rites seem expressions of pure lunacy; at closer scrutiny they become nauseatingly repulsive. They picture an exaggerated confidence between individuals, or at least between certain individuals. This in itself I consider treasonable. The too gullible one will sooner or later experience the same fate as their hero Reor—sooner or later he will be robbed and murdered. *And is this not the very reason for the establishment of the State?* If there were cause and reason for confidence among individuals, the State would never have come into existence. The sacred and essential foundation for the State is our mutual and well-founded suspicion of each other. Anyone questioning this foundation throws suspicion upon the State."

"Nonsense!" said Rissen, with a certain annoyance. "You seem to forget that it would exist anyway, as an economic and cultural center . . ."

"I'm not forgetting that," I said. "And please do not think my opinion originates from some civilian superstition that the State exists for our sake, instead of we for the State's, as is indeed the fact. I only mean that the kernel of the matter, the individual cell's relationship to the state-organism, lies in the hunger for security. If one day we should notice—I do not say we have done so but *if*—if we should notice that our pea soup is thinner, our soap hardly usable, our apartments ready to fall to pieces, and nobody doing anything about it—would we then complain? No! We know that comfortable living is of no value in itself, that our sacrifices serve a higher purpose. If we should discover barbed wire across our streets, wouldn't we endure all restrictions to our freedom of movement without complaint? Of course we would! We would know that this was done for the State's sake, to stop enemies. And if one day we should discover that all our free-time occupations had been curtailed for necessary military duty, that the many expectations and experiences of luxury which were part of our upbringing, now must be put aside for an unavoidable concentration of everyone's special skills in essential industry—would we then have reason to complain? No, no, and again no! We realize, and approve, that the State is all, the individual nothing. We realize and admit that most of the so-called 'culture'—aside from purely technical knowledge—must remain a luxury for times when no danger threatens (times which perhaps never will come again). What remains is life's bare essentials and the ever more highly developed military and police activities. This is the kernel of the State's life. Everything else is superficial."

Rissen kept his silence, dark and thoughtful. Perhaps he had difficulty in finding objections to my not too original theme, but I was sure—and enjoyed it—that his civilian soul grumbled in annoyance.

Karrek had jumped to his feet and was walking back and forth. I had an impression that he had not been listening too closely to my arguments and this bothered me. When I concluded, he said, with some impatience, "Yes, yes, that's well and good. The fact is, however, that as far as I know we've had no fight against 'spirits' before. We have left them to their own ghostly activities in the spheres where they belong. When people say something they shouldn't at the supper table, or play hooky from festivities, at least it's something you can deal with, but 'spirits'—no, thank you!"

"Until now we have never had any means to deal with them," I retorted. "Kallocain offers us the possibility of controlling what goes on in people's minds."

But he did not seem, this time either, to listen to my argument with more than half an ear.

"Anyone might be condemned with that," he said, with a touch of anger in his voice.

Suddenly he was silent, struck, it seemed, with the implication in his own words.

"Anyone might be condemned with that," he repeated, but this time with infinite slowness, his voice low and soft. "In any case, perhaps you are not so far wrong, when all is said and done—when *all is said* and done . . ."

"But if you yourself, my Chief," exclaimed Rissen, horrified, "if you say that anyone . . ."

Karrek, however, did not listen to him either; he had

resumed his pacing back and forth with long strides, his strange, Mongolian head, with the narrow eyes, bent forward.

I wanted to play up to him; so I started to tell, although with a certain feeling of shame, about the reprimand I had received from the Propaganda Ministry's Seventh Bureau. This caught his attention at last.

"You say the Propaganda Ministry's Seventh Bureau?" he repeated, thoughtfully. "That is interesting. That is very interesting."

A long time elapsed while the sound of his faintly squeaking soles was the only thing heard, except for the distant, changing rumble of the subway and the hum of voices and other commotion from nearby rooms. Finally he leaned against the wall, supported by his hand, closed his eyes, and said slowly, as if weighing every word, "Let me be completely honest; it is in our power to get through such a law, about criminality of the mind, if we have a sufficient connection with the Seventh Bureau."

I do believe all I was doing then was playing up to Karrek, but it is possible that I also became contaminated a little by his dreams of greatness, by plans and visions unknown to me. Anyway, I held my breath when he continued, "I wish to send one of you to the Seventh Bureau, one who can speak with persuasion. For certain reasons I can't go myself. How about you, Fellow-Soldier Kall? Can you put your words well? But let me ask your chief. Can he, Fellow-Soldier Rissen?"

Only after a moment's hesitation did Rissen reply, almost reluctantly, "He can, in highest degree."

This was the first time I had noticed a decided antagonism on Rissen's part.

"Let me talk with you alone then, Fellow-Soldier Kall."

We withdrew to my cubicle. With utter disrespect

Karrek pushed a pillow into the police-ear, and as he noticed my surprised reaction, he said, with a laugh, "Well, I am a chief of police myself and if against all odds anyone should discover it, I know where I have Tuareg."

I could not help but admire him in his very impudence, but it bothered me a little that he was so completely dominated by personal connections rather than principles.

"Well, then," he said, "you must find an excuse to talk with Lavris in the Seventh Bureau. I suggest you take up that reprimand you spoke of and connect it with your discovery in some way. And then in passing—remember well, *in passing*, since lawmaking as such does not come under the Seventh Bureau—you must mention how great an importance it would have with our new law—yours and mine. . . . I must explain to you—Lavris has influence with Law Minister Tatjo."

"But wouldn't it be more practical to go directly to Law Minister Tatjo?"

"On the contrary, extremely impractical. Even if you had a definite errand, a bona fide errand as compared to a suggestion for a law, it would take weeks before you could be admitted to him, and we can't do without you for so long a time in Chemistry City No. 4. And if you alone came with the law-petition it's doubtful if you ever would be admitted. Who are you, they would ask, to suggest new laws? The individual obeys the laws, he does not make them. If Lavris, however, gets hold of the matter . . . But the idea is to get her interested. Do you think you can?"

"The worst I can do is fail," I said. "I'm not exposing myself to any danger."

Within myself I felt convinced I would succeed; it was exactly the type of mission where I could use my best capabilities. Karrek must have realized this as his probing eyes rested on me.

"Good luck then!" he said. "I'll have your license by tomorrow, and also some recommendations. Now I give you permission to return to your work."

We had to wait for Tuareg. To somebody accustomed to a definite use for each and every minute, day and night, such an empty time-lapse can be extremely painful; but everything, even the worst, will pass, and at last the police minister came, so that we could show him what the Kallocain was worth. I had hardly imagined that I would have to control myself so intensely in order not to let my hand tremble when the sleeve was turned up on the arm of an unshaven, criminal type in the chair before me, but Tuareg's narrow bear-eyes pierced me in the back so sharply that I almost felt it was I who was getting the needle. But all progressed as it should; between strings of indecencies, which brought a slight smile to the police minister's full lips and thus eased the tension a little, the test-person not only made a full confession of the crime he was accused of but so far had escaped conviction for, he also admitted a great many other crimes, perpetrated alone or with others. Without hesitation he divulged all names and details. Tuareg's nostrils quivered with pleasure.

We continued with others. Rissen and I took turns with the needle, the police minister's secretary in person took down the confessions, and in order to further test us an occasional innocent fellow-soldier had been placed among the others—that is to say, innocent as far as crime was concerned; in another sense the word could never have been more wrongly used, to the minister's apparent enjoyment. After we had examined six people in a remarkably short time, Tuareg rose and said he was fully convinced; Kallocain would speedily replace all other methods of investigation used in the Worldstate, he declared. He wished to keep us for a few days to train some of the experts in the Capital; furthermore, he wished to announce that when we returned home our duty would be to instruct injectors from all parts of the State, as well as to teach Kallocain-makers in great numbers from the chemistry cities. He left us with all indications of his good will, and shortly afterward some twenty persons showed up whom we apparently were to instruct. Test-persons lined up outside the door, all criminals directly from jail.

The very next day I was summoned to Karrek and was ordered to leave all the work to Rissen for the time being. I was handed a large sheaf of papers, containing licenses, recommendations, and identifications of various kinds.

I believe I have forgotten to say that the petition I had formulated and circulated through the various laboratories in Chemistry City, concerning propaganda for the Voluntary Sacrificial Service, had been signed in full within a few days and I had brought all these signatures with me in order to present them personally to the Propaganda Ministry. To be on the safe side I had asked Karrek to whom I ought to direct myself and he had given me good advice. My excellent recommendations would surely also be useful at the Third Bureau, where such propaganda originated. Soon I was sitting on the Metro, and presently I stepped off at the Propaganda Ministry's imposing underground portals.

Early that morning I had felt a slight indisposition coming on, and the police ministry's personnel-doctor had poured diverse preparations down my throat, so that my condition was rather abnormal. Perhaps this was the reason why I felt so inexplicably excited when I asked for an audience with Lavris, Chief of the Seventh Bureau. Actually I was on Karrek's errands more than my own, since it was he who had shown so much interest in having this new law effectuated, for reasons unknown to me. But in my exalted condition I had a feeling I was not acting on Karrek's behalf, nor on my own, rather that my doings were a link in the immense State-evolution, perhaps the last step before perfection was reached. I, an unimportant cell in the great State organism (in my own person poisoned, moreover, even if only momentarily, by multitudes of pills and powders), was busy undertaking a cleansing procedure that would rid the State's body of all the sickening poison the thought-violators injected. When at last—after many formalities, a complete bodily search, and a long wait—I rose to be admitted to Lavris' reception room, I felt as if walking to my own purgation, from which I would emerge completely calm and free from all the asocial dregs I did not wish to acknowledge but which lurked so insidiously in the dark corners of my mind and which I could summarize with one word: Rissen.

Nothing in Lavris' room set it apart from a thousand other workrooms, except for the guards with raised guns who were posted here as they had been with the police minister, indicating that the person working here was one of the State's rare and valuable tools. Yet, I felt breathless and my temples kept pulsating. The tall, thin-necked woman behind the desk, her skin stretched over lips and cheeks in a permanent ironic smile, was Kalipso Lavris.

Even if her age had not been indefinite and her bearing stiff as in an ancient idol I might still, in my feverish condition, have taken her as only half human. Not even an enormous pimple on the left side of her nose, just about to reach its full ripeness, could pull her down to earth in my eyes. Did she not function as the Worldstate's highest ethical authority? Or at least as the leading force in the Worldstate's highest ethical authority, which indeed the Propaganda Ministry's Seventh Bureau was! In her face one could not read anything personal, as with Tuareg; her immobility held in check no secret springs, as with Karrek; to me she seemed the crystal-clear personification of logic, cleansed of individuality's incidentals. This was a fever-fantasy, yet for all its exaggeration it caught Lavris' picture rather strikingly, I suspect.

I had been warned that any reference to a change in the law must not be made directly, since the Seventh Bureau had nothing to do with this officially. The guards with their raised guns reminded me still further, yet without disturbing me. My errand was a necessity in order that the State, that I, would not perish.

I do not know exactly how I brought up the old reprimand. While my secret police card was being examined I had to wait in a special little waiting room, almost two hours, I believe. One must learn this, I thought, one must learn to wait. And I managed. Yet I must admit the examination was quickly expedited when one realized what enormous space such a card system must occupy, covering every fellow-soldier of the Worldstate. Even though I never have seen this complex I can well imagine it must take at least an hour to reach the room where my card was. On the other hand, obviously everything must be so systematically organized that no long time would be required once the room had been reached. But then the long way back again. Realizing further that the card system probably was not kept at the Propaganda Ministry but rather at the Police Department, I felt I had small reason to complain over my two hours.

When I was readmitted, Lavris was studying my card ("card," by the way, is a misnomer; actually it resembled a small book) and a thin stack of papers, probably the preparations and the reports concerning my reprimand. It was quite evident that she had forgotten my case, so occupied as the Seventh Bureau must be with the most amazing reports and cases from all parts of the World-state.

"Well," said Lavris, in her toneless and yet high voice. "Here we have your case. It says on your police card you have already asked to make an apology over the radio, but have as yet not had the opportunity. What exactly do you want?"

"I have kept in mind the words: *the disclosure of the former* (the splintered ones) *is a commendable action for the State's welfare,*" I said. "I have even made a discovery that will bring about their disclosure more effectively and more systematically than before."

And I explained the Kallocain as enlighteningly as I could.

"Now," I concluded, "one only has to wait for a new law, of a kind probing more deeply than the world has known hitherto: a law against treasonable thoughts and feelings. Perhaps it will take some time, but I feel sure it'll come."

She did not seem to react to my feeler; I decided to try the same words that took with Karrek.

"Anyone can be condemned under that law," I said, insinuatingly, and added only after a long pause: "Of course, I mean anyone not completely loyal to the bottom of his heart."

Lavris sat silent and thoughtful; the skin over her cheek bones perhaps stretched a bit, and suddenly she lifted her long, well-formed hand, picked up a pencil gingerly between her index finger and thumb and squeezed it slowly until her knuckles whitened. Without letting go her hold she looked up again and asked, "Was this your whole errand, Fellow-Soldier?"

"It is my whole errand," I replied. "Only to make the Seventh Bureau aware of a discovery that will show criminal inner splintering, even though such splintering is not as yet a crime in the eyes of the law. If I have usurped the Bureau's time needlessly I am willing to apologize."

"The Seventh Bureau thanks you for your good intention," she replied, with ice-cold impenetrability.

I saluted and left, filled with doubt, and still shivering with fever.

As I stumbled in to the Third Bureau with my lists of signatures, the clock struck an end to the workday and I was almost trampled down by the outrushing crowd. One older, morose-looking man remained behind to finish some calculations, and I felt I could do no better than turn to him. He wrinkled his nose, controlled his sour disposition when he saw my recommendations, looked over the lists, and said, "One thousand two hundred names, did you say? All scientifically worthy? What a pity you are too late. Your petition happens to have been granted before you even had time to present it. From no less than seven other chemistry cities the same petitions have come in, some already eight months ago. Propaganda of the type you wish is already being prepared."

"Nothing can please me more," I said, a little disappointed that I myself had no part in this worthy activity.

"Consequently you have no business here," said the man, and went back to his number columns.

"But couldn't I take part in some way?" I pleaded, seized with a pride no doubt caused by the fever. "When I can prove how interested I am in this work couldn't I help some with the preparations? I have a lot of recommendations—look here—and see these—and these here—"

He glanced for one moment at my imposing papers, then again at his unfinished column; finally he stared with a sigh after the last of his fellow workers disappearing through the door. He dared not send me away. At last he took the solution which seemed to him least time-consuming:

"I'll give you a pass," he said, and wrote a few lines on a typewriter, grabbed the enormous seal of the Third Bureau, stamped what he had written, and handed me the paper.

"The Film Studio Palace at 20 o'clock this evening," he said. "I don't know what they're up to but it must be something. I'm sure you'll get in. No one knows me, but they recognize the stamp.—Are you satisfied now? I only hope I haven't done something I shouldn't have. . . ."

I felt almost sure he had done something wrong. A few days later it was made quite clear to me that properly I never should have been given access to the Film Studio Palace. It became obvious that a quite different preparation would have been necessary for me, perhaps an entirely different education from mine, in order to avoid the shock I received here; and consequently I was also sure that the right authorities would have resolutely denied me attendance. Possibly the impressions became somewhat distorted in my still persisting feverish condition; but such distortions normally disappear quickly enough, whereas the shock I received during my evening visit to the Film Palace left scars for weeks afterwards.

My determined dwelling-in-the-world-of-higher-principles was cut short. Lavris' impenetrable coldness had shaken my self-confidence, perhaps above all the belief in myself. Who was I to come with plans to save the State? A sick, tired individual, too sick and tired to find refuge in irreproachable ethical principles expressed in a high and toneless voice. Lavris should have had a deep, motherly voice, like that woman in the lunatic sect; she should have comforted like Linda, she should have been a quite ordinary, friendly woman. . . . Having reached this far I jumped up from my half-slumber and got off at the right Metro-station. The late-working official's pass with the Third Bureau's stamp served as my license, and without knowing exactly how, I found myself at the subterranean gate which led to the Film Palace. In the Capital all buildings of importance had their subterranean entrances, and that is how it happened that never during my stay there did I have a chance to get above ground.

When I had followed my whim and asked to participate, it had been with the thought in mind that I might be allowed to see the making of a film. This would have been most interesting, and would have required just about the right effort for the condition I was in—to sit in a more or less comfortable chair and watch the filming of a scene. But I had misjudged. The room to which I was admitted was an ordinary lecture hall; no klieg lights, no scenery, no costumes were in sight; there were about one hundred people in the audience, all in leisure-time uniforms, that was all. I was questioned in detail as to who I was, all my papers were inspected, and finally I was ushered to a seat near the back.

The speeches of greetings began. As far as I could deduce, this was a meeting to examine in rough outline a number of manuscripts that had come in, agree upon the lines of the desired play, and begin a first sorting of the material. A number of institutions were named as being contributors, among them several of the Propaganda Ministry's bureaus, the Advisory Committee of the Artists, and the Ministry of Health. The Voluntary Sacrificial Service, however, was not represented—a fact which I was better able to understand than most. Then the evening's lecturer was introduced, a psychology specialist in the field, it seemed. I looked at him with great curiosity as he stepped up on the podium. Psychologists were hardly known in the chemistry cities, discounting a few advisors at child- and youth-camps and the psycho-technicians who performed the necessary tests when the youths were sorted out for their various vocations. Djin Kakumita was a short, thin man, with black hair, very lively and adroit in all his gestures. When I attempt to repeat his introduction word for word, I realize full well that it is impossible and that many passages elude my memory. Yet I feel the picture is still clear enough for me to give an idea as to the contents.

"Fellow-Soldiers!" he began. "Before me I have a stack of manuscripts which have originated with no fewer than three hundred and seventy-two film authors. It would be unreasonable to expect a detailed description of each of the three hundred and seventy-two manuscripts in an introduction for a discussion—I apologize to authors possibly present." (Laughter in the audience: obviously none of these beginning writers had been invited to participate in the shaping of the finished product although they supplied the raw material as it were.) "Instead, I will make a short general criticism and at the same time offer a line of direction for the work.

"To begin with, I've taken the liberty of dividing these stories into two main groups: those with a 'happy' ending, and those with an 'unhappy' ending. Since the purpose is to entice and induce, one might be inclined to believe that the ones with a happy ending would best serve the purpose. Such, however, is not the case, as I will proceed to show. For whom is a happy ending an enticement? For those who are dull in their reactions, for those who, when all is said and done, actually fear pain and death; and we are not directing ourselves to them. Psychological investigations have shown that the Voluntary Sacrificial Service gains singularly few recruits among them. When that type of people finally arrive at the happy ending, they have forgotten the real meaning of the film. They go home and sleep sweetly, as usual assured that now both the hero and the heroine are well off. They don't go to the propaganda office and offer their services. Sacrificial Service films with happy endings are for the in-between times, not for the campaign periods. They are there to calm and cheer relatives and other fellow-soldiers, if perchance they should happen to think of children, brothers, sisters, comrades who have disappeared in the Voluntary Sacrificial Service. Such films should be shown only occasionally, and to have a really good effect they should not only end happily, they should have a strong element of sunny humor, ribaldry, also touching moments, but not heroic. In this respect one group of manuscripts falls between two stools so to speak: they offer an unhappy mixture of desirable between-drives mentality and the mentality that should come to the fore at drive-periods.

"The films which have proven to be most effective have always been those with a so-called unhappy ending. I say 'so-called,' since it always remains arbitrary as to what one might consider the greatest happiness for the individual—arbitrary and yet of no consequence since in the final analysis nothing ought to be considered from the point of view of the individual. I am referring to films where the hero is crushed. Under all circumstances we can count on a certain percentage of fellow-soldiers to whom this self-immolation seems the highest bliss, and especially if it is for the State. It is from this percentage that the Voluntary Sacrificial Service mainly is recruited, and I have reasons to believe—reasons which I will come back to later—that this percentage is particularly high in our days. Our task, then, is only to awaken and sharpen the tendencies that are there already and drive them in the right direction.

"As a rule, however, heroes-to-be (in real life) are a little particular as to the choice of their destruction. We must portray a doom that captivates. First of all, we must avoid sicknesses and ways of dying that have something ridiculous about them; situations where the test-person becomes a wreck, unable to hold on to his dignity, unable to control himself, unable to help himself concerning the simplest biological needs; such situations are to be avoided in films of this sort. For between-drives films, all right! And then with a happy ending, and emphasis on the comical side. But the sufferings which will tempt heroes must (*a*) be *dignified* in appearance, and (*b*) have a *purpose*.

"The longing to feel oneself exclusively a tool for a higher purpose is a force to take into account far beyond the limits of the heroic type I have talked about so far. No one can seriously believe that his own life has a value in itself as such. If we are to speak of the value of life, it must of necessity concern a value outside the individual. Which day, which hour of our life dare we conceive valuable in itself? None. And I maintain that this consciousness of the individual life's valuelessness creates within us an ever stronger consciousness of the Higher Purpose and its all-overshadowing demand; in other words: a dawning of State-consciousness in the brains of the fellow-soldiers. The suffering which a motion picture portrays must consequently have a superindividual gain as result—it must not be *one* person who is saved through the destruction of the hero—then he might as well have saved himself!—nor even a smaller number, but thousands, millions, *preferably all the fellow-soldiers of the World-state*.

"A subdivision of this purposefulness is (*c*) the *quality of glory* in the destruction that is portrayed. With this I do not mean that the hero ought to reap positive glory; this would lower the film's level and immediately have a weaker effect on truly heroic natures. Conversely, he should be spared deep inner disgrace. For against the hero one usually contrasts the villain who is asocial and has selfish motives, the man who falls into temptation and avoids pain and death. Coarsely ugly or unsympathetically smooth-looking, soft and undisciplined, a coward, a

117

waster—he should be a continuous warning parallel through his actions, yet never too exaggerated in type, lest he fail to pierce like a thorn in sensitive minds: *you* wouldn't be one of these? The fear of being a coward, without honor, ugly in an inner sense, is indeed often a strongly driving force in the heroic type I have described here, and whom we must above all aim for, in our propaganda campaign.

"Very few of the manuscripts I have before me meet the stringent requirements I have set forth. Our further work will indeed be instructive: we must divide the material between a number of study groups, along the lines I have laid down, sort it and criticize it, and what is usable must be forged together, be improved, sharpened, until we have a comparatively small number of suggestions, all of which are fully satisfactory. This work should be completed in two weeks, and then we will meet again and start to examine the result together. Thank you for your attention, and let's have a lively discussion."

He stepped down from the podium. I felt strangely depressed, although I could not say why. I was sure that everybody around me felt it nothing but inspiring that he had talked about the fellow-soldiers the way a clever technician speaks of a complexly functioning mechanism; I felt sure they were fired by his superiority and felt that they themselves were in control of the machine and pulled the levers. But whether it was caused by the fever or not, I did have an all too vivid impression of my first test-person, No. 135, and of his one great moment, which I had envied him. I might despise No. 135 as much as I pleased, I could treat him as badly as I wished in my thoughts or in reality, but as long as I envied him I could not look upon him as an engineer does his machine.

The discussion began. Someone pointed out the importance of making the heroes in most films young, in order to appeal to youth. Not because it was so much more *desirable* to have younger members in the Sacrificial Service. The statistics indicated that a test-person on the average lasted just so many years, regardless of the age at which he was first used, and it might therefore even be said that it would be a pure advantage if the state could have *first* a few years work out of him in some other capacity, and *later* the statistical average number of years in the Sacrificial Service, instead of *only* these final years. But another point weighed heavier: it was so much easier to sway youth. Marriage and a busy work-life as a rule had a most adverse effect on the number of volunteers for sacrificial work. Admittedly, within all groups and all ages there were 'loners' who hungered for they did not know what, and when the thing called happiness and the thing called life had failed them, they were ready to try the direct opposite in order perhaps to have better luck there, and they must not be overlooked. But the formative years —especially well-organized formative years—were after all the years of loneliness and disappointment above others—or perhaps only the years of *audacious* loneliness and disappointment?—and consequently one ought to aim at them before others.

Somebody else underlined the last speaker's opinions and added that youth offered still another advantage over mature age: since such a great number of volunteers streamed in from the youth-camps after each well-organized campaign, one had an opportunity to choose. Because it would be senseless to accept all, lock, stock, and barrel. Many had such potentialities that the State could well use their brains rather than their tissues and bodily members. One must also take into consideration that the minimal age must not be set too low; before fifteen, or sixteen, it would be hazardous to judge their general and special use.

One extreme speaker objected to this last opinion and declared that one could already in an eight-year-old discern if he were a specially gifted child, worthy of consideration or not, and one could therefore well lower the minimum age to eight for volunteer service; indeed, why not make a few films especially adapted to that age group? In contradiction to him several other speakers pointed out that examples were abundant of gifted natures of great use that had not been apparent before a much later age; also, an appeal to the child's age-group would not be of sufficient importance to justify the great cost of special films. To be sure, something would be saved among those children who volunteered, since they never would require any further education, but on the other hand, only in puberty did heroic inclinations *of this sort* actually blossom.

Someone else pointed out the importance of showing these films at shorter intervals. Special pressure was not considered desirable to obtain volunteers, nor was it necessary. A certain surprise was thought to have almost the same effect as force and to be in the long run less damaging. No harm in forcing to a quick decision: Now or never! If not within such or such time it will be too late! The anxiety which is liable to arise at certain definite crises in life is sharpened by an urgent choice and impels one in the right direction, if the propaganda is well presented.

Someone expressed thanks for the last viewpoint and emphasized that this anxiety, which now and again rose within every fellow-soldier, could become an invaluable asset to the State, if experienced psychologists were to handle it. When it worked, so to speak, as a postulate for a decision it did not matter at all if the decision was rather fateful; the increased relaxation after it was made and the ecstatic joy in the first volunteer attracted others in much greater numbers than if the whole matter were treated as inconsequential. To make the decision irrevocable was to aim a little too high, even the now obligatory ten years was too much, thought the speaker. Precisely the same effect could be gained, with less apprehension, if the volunteer period were lowered to five years. Already after five years the test-person seldom possessed youth, strength, or possibilities to choose a new life. Propaganda, then, if well presented, should avoid all force and consequently all resistance.

Bear in mind, I was sick with fever. In no other way can it be explained that I rose and asked to be heard. Strangely enough, No. 135 must still have been haunting my brain; when I had him in my power I had done all I could to humiliate him, but now it seemed I must speak in his behalf.

"I must voice a complaint against your attitude towards your fellow-soldiers in treating them like mechanisms," I began, slowly and haltingly. "It seems to me it shows lack of consideration—respect . . ."

My voice failed me and I felt too confused to choose the right words and speak convincingly.

"Not at all!" shouted one of the earlier speakers, impatiently. "What are you trying to insinuate! No one places a higher value on the heroic type than I. Shouldn't I know how important he is to the State—I who have spent many years of my life in the study of just that type and his qualifications! Do you think I would have done so had I considered him valueless? And then you come and speak of lack of respect!"

"Yes! Yes!" I shouted, confused. "Respect for the result, but—but . . ."

"But what?" asked my antagonist when I grew silent. "What is it I don't have respect for?"

"Nothing," I said, weakly, and sat down. "You are right. I was mistaken and apologize."

I had stopped at the right moment, I noticed, with the

cold perspiration on my forehead. What had I intended to say? "You lack respect for No. 135 in person?" Pretty opinions. Secret individualistic currents below the surface. I was afraid of myself.

No, not of myself! It was not I, this that I detested and fought. It was not I. It was Rissen.

For a long moment I could hear nothing of what went on around me, so shaken was I from the danger I had escaped. When at last I managed to concentrate, Djin Kakumita had again ascended the podium. I gathered that he had been speaking for some time.

"This so-called passive heroic type," he was saying, "is indeed more and more in demand within the State's function. Not only is he necessary within the Voluntary Sacrificial Service, but also as the average individual in the line of duty, as a subordinate official, as bearer and deliverer of children to the State, in a thousand and one posts. The need becomes especially strong in time of war, when each or every second soldier ought to belong to this group. On the other hand it must be obvious to anyone that he is not desirable in a leading position, where a cold, objective view, quick action, and ruthless force are demanded. The problem might be put this way: How, in time of need, can one increase the number of this the most noble of all types, this desperate and lonely hero-soul, disappointed with life and anxious for pain and death? Well . . ."

I felt indeed very sick and decided to leave the hall. Since I was a stranger and did not belong to any of the working-groups, it could make no difference actually. With slow, silent steps, in order to disturb as little as possible, I stole towards the door, where I showed my papers to the guard and in a whisper tried to explain my behavior. While so doing I was interrupted by a tall, dark-complexioned man in police- and military-uniform with remarkably high insignia. Strangely enough, he had come from outside to enter the hall at this late hour. He showed a paper to the guard who not only admitted him at once but even accompanied him down the aisle, so that I without further ado could get out into the corridor. From inside I could hear a low, firm voice, but could not distinguish what was said, and when it stopped, a rising hum of voices from the audience.

Just then the guard returned to his post and I could not help but ask him what was happening.

"Ssh!" he whispered, and looked about. "Since you were one of them anyway I will tell you, Fellow-Soldier: the making of propaganda films for the Voluntary Sacrificial Service has been cancelled. All available manpower is needed elsewhere. You know what that means, and I know too, but none of us has the right to know it aloud...."

To express oneself in such a manner was already to know it aloud, yet I did not feel inclined to start trouble, tired as I was. But he was right: I knew very well what the cancellation meant. The Worldstate was in the shadow of a new war.

My longing for adventure had been satisfied. My experiences in the Capital had been sufficiently various and instructive that I was sure never to forget them: the ultimate test of the Kallocain before Tuareg, my call at the Seventh Bureau, and last but not least the psychological discussion of films for which I was not ripe. No, indeed, I was not ripe for it; it stayed with me and gnawed like a hidden ulcer. Yet, there was nothing I could object to in a single statement—the purely psychological assertions I must leave to the experts—and I felt terribly humiliated every time I thought of my uncalled-for and stupid interruption. Since I had fully understood their point of view, why, then, did I continue to be tortured by it? Probably never before had I heard it stated so clearly, so to the point, how objectively the value of each fellow-soldier's contribution must be seen; and yet I felt as if the troubles of existence were gigantic and the meaning of it all was evanescent and trivial. I knew this was a false and unhealthy view, and I tried to convince myself with all possible arguments. But for the desolate emptiness that grew within me I could find no other name than *meaninglessness*.

What a joke, I thought with horror, if some policeman, or perhaps Rissen, had taken the needle from my hand and pushed it into my own arm instead. What the Seventh Bureau would have said about my state of mind was easy to imagine. Had Rissen only had the right he would probably with pleasure have offered to unmask me, I thought, and discover further proof of his old statement: "No fellow-soldier over forty has a clear conscience." Wasn't that what he had wished right along? Wasn't it he who actually had brought me thus far with his sly insinuations? The man was a threat to me and to all. Most horrible was my worry over how far he might have brought Linda with him towards destruction, and whether the two of them were in league against me.

All this was seething under the surface. But externally I had too much to do to devote my time to worries. Tuareg had already ordered the usual court procedure to be replaced with Kallocain tests, and people from all over the Worldstate were already streaming in to attend the new courses we had been instructed to arrange. We were transferred—temporarily, it was said—to the police department and were given space in the police department complex. All arrested persons were sent directly to our lecture halls by Karrek, so that they could be processed and act as test material simultaneously. In consequence, there was always present some higher military or police officer who acted as judge, and both the police secretary and such secretaries as we had appointed took down the records.

It soon became apparent that the work was growing over our heads. We were forced to admit more participants in the courses than was suitable, and yet many had to wait. Nor did we have time to examine all arrested persons, although we rushed from case to case, even had to cut short our mealtimes.

The courts' activities, moreover, had from time immemorial been secret, and therefore I had nothing with which to compare. But it struck me that so many of the accusations were false, or in any case unnecessary. Practically every one of the respondents stumbled out of the room crushed and broken—without cause, one might almost say, after having become casehardened by several hundred excuses and explanations from more or less foolish fellow-soldiers—and yet their disclosures were often of so ridiculously unimportant a nature, from the judicial point of view, that I was beginning to wonder if the apparatus was worth its price. Complications arose also with the Kallocain, which was still manufactured in limited quantities in the laboratory.

Once we happened to discuss the problem at the dinner table ("we" being Rissen and I, and all participants in the course, who had been given tables in the large dining room where the police personnel also took their meals). We had, as usual, been terribly rushed during the forenoon, the air had been more humid and hot than usual, and on top of it all, some of our air-conditioning units failed to function. Someone was complaining aloud about the many accusations involving unimportant matters or nothing at all.

"The accusations have increased steadily for the last twenty years," said Rissen. "The chief of police told me so himself."

"But that need not mean that crime has increased," I said. "It might just as well mean that loyalty has increased, a consciousness of where rottenness exists . . ."

"It means that fear has increased," said Rissen, with unexpected heat.

"Fear?"

"Yes, fear. We have developed towards ever stricter supervision, and it has not made us more secure, as we had hoped, but rather more insecure. With our fear grows also our impulse to strike out. Isn't it true that when a beast is threatened and sees no way of escape, it attacks. When fear steals over us there is nothing to do but strike first. It's difficult since we don't even know in which direction to strike. . . . But better attack than be attacked —isn't that an old saying? If one strikes often enough and hard enough perhaps one may save oneself. There is an old joke about a fencer who was so dexterous he managed to keep dry when it rained: he swung his sword against the falling raindrops and prevented them from falling on him. Somewhat in the same manner must we fence, we who happen to be caught in the great fear."

"You speak as if everyone had something to hide," I said, but I could hear for myself how lame it sounded, how little convincing. Although I did not wish to believe him, I could, against my will, see a sight that frightened me. *If*, after all, he were right, and if my errand with Lavris bore fruit, if not only words and actions but also thoughts and feelings were to be examined and judged— then, then . . . Like crawling ants in an anthill all fellow-soldiers would get busy, however not like the ants to work together, but to forestall each other. I could see them mill about: fellow-workers reporting fellow-workers, husbands their wives, and wives husbands, subordinates accusing their chiefs, and chiefs their subordinates. . . . Rissen must not be proven right. I hated him because he had the power to force his thoughts on me. But I relaxed as I visualized who would be the first victim if the new law became a reality.

A few days later came an order from Karrek that the course should be divided. The continued judicial examinations with accompanying instruction would be led by Rissen, aided by more advanced students. I, on the other hand, would head a special chemistry course to facilitate Kallocain manufacture on a greater scale.

The need called for it, I realized. And I should have been happy to return to chemistry. But the order annoyed me and made me feel disappointed.

And this had its cause as follows.

On our list of persons to be examined we had still the old man from the lunatic sect whom I spoke about earlier and whom we had been ready to examine before our journey to the Capital. As it happened, his case had been delayed; he had become ill and had only just recovered. His name was on the list for tomorrow, just when I was to start my new chemistry course. It surprised me, almost frightened me, that I was so disappointed at not being able to be present at that examination. I had to ask myself if I was expecting something similar to that woman who had made such a deep impression on me; was I attracted by a new exposure to similar dangerous influences? But why need I resort to degrading reasons; my interest was surely first and foremost the whole sorry mess, which Karrek had ordered us to wind up—I wanted to know what was the kernel of truth behind all those insanities. The man's intelligent appearance had led me to believe he might be more initiated into the gang's deepest secrets than anyone we had interrogated earlier. I was anxious to be present at that unmasking, especially as I suspected Rissen of shady sympathies. There was indeed also a negative interest, I told myself, which had nothing whatsoever to do with positive interest: was my interest in the lunatic sect identical with my interest in Rissen?

Even though I had to obey orders I promised myself I would not completely lose contact with this case.

"Is it permissible to ask if that sick man was examined today?" I said, the following day at dinner.

"Yes, he was examined today," said Rissen, curtly.

"And what came out? Anything criminal?"

"He was convicted."

"For what?"

"He was considered a threat to the State."

It was impossible to get anything definite from my chief; I could see no way out except to ask to see the report.

"I have no authority to permit or deny this," said Rissen. "That's up to the chief of police."

Karrek made no objections when I asked him over the telephone. And so, on my first free evening, I went to the police department, where Rissen was waiting for me, to unlock the safe and hand me the document. It was the course-report (the police-report was kept somewhere else, I don't know where), and it was very detailed. I had to read it right there, and at first it bothered me that Rissen had work to do there just that evening; he wanted to make explanations and give further information, which I did not wish.

But after I had started reading I changed my mind; since he was so close by I might as well let him talk.

"This I would like to know something more about," I said. " 'The examined person started to utter strange songs.' What does that mean? In what way were they strange?"

Rissen shrugged his shoulders.

"They simply were," he said. "They were not like anything I've heard. Vague words only, metaphors and images, I believe—and melodies, but I can't see how any soldiers in the world could march to them. . . . But they made a strong impression on me and I seldom have been so moved."

His voice trembled so noticeably that his emotion was close to affecting me also. I should never have come here; I should have been warned by the warm woman-voice which had spoken of the "organic" and had created a sort of mirage in my mind, an enduring mirage of deepest rest. This vision suddenly came alive again, and it struck me as something quite unjust, sly and demoniacal, that an inner contagion can be transferred, not only directly but also indirectly—from that unknown man whose singing I had not heard, and to me, as an echo, through Rissen's voice.

"Could you give me some idea about his songs?" I asked, unsteadily. "Could you repeat them?"

But he shook his head. "They were too strange. They only stupefied me."

I continued my reading and made an effort to get away from this feeling which I hated.

"You yourself must admit this is criminal," I said. "As far as I know, *all* geographical information and rumors are treasonable. And this: *a deserted city of ruins in an inaccessible place!* An unknown and unreachable desert city! As I see, he wasn't able to give the exact location. But even to spread such hints!"

"Who knows whether or not it exists, that desert city?" said Rissen, dubiously. "He himself insisted it was known only to a few chosen ones, and some of those lived in the ruins. Why need it be more than a legend!"

"In that case a criminal legend, since after all it's a geographical rumor. *If* now such a desert city should exist, and *if*, as he says, it is a remnant from the days before the great world wars and before the Worldstate, and *if* it actually was destroyed by bombs and gas and bacteria—how would anyone dare live there, even if he were a lunatic? If it contained any possibility of sustaining life, the State would long ago have taken it over."

"If you look a little further on in the record," said Rissen, "you'll see it is said to be still dangerous; in places the very stones and the sand are said to contain poisonous evaporations; bacteria have kept alive in crevices and cracks; indeed, every step is hazardous. But as you also can see, he says there are fresh springs and there is uncontaminated soil in which to cultivate vegetables, and the few inhabitants know the passable paths and the hiding places and live in friendship and mutual help."

"I see, yes. A miserable, insecure life, full of anxiety. But an instructive legend: such must life be—constant anxiety and danger—if one flees the great communion, the State."

He was silent. I continued to read and could not help but sigh and shake my head.

"A legend!" I said. "A saga of something that doesn't exist! The remnants of a dead civilization! In that gas-infested desert hole they are supposed to keep alive the remnants of a dead civilization from the time before the great wars! There was no such civilization!"

With a jerk Rissen turned towards me. "How can you be so sure of that?" he asked.

I stared at him in surprise. "But that much we have at least learned even as children," I said. "Nothing worthy of the name civilization can be imagined to have existed during the civilian-individualistic epoch. Private groups fought private groups, community groups other community groups. Valuable forces, strong arms, excellent brains could at will be put aside, pushed down by an antagonist, be denied access to work, fade away unused and without purpose. . . . Such I call a jungle, but not civilization."

"I too," agreed Rissen, seriously. "And yet, yet . . . couldn't one imagine a spring, a subterranean spring, overlooked, that would break to the surface in the jungle also?"

"Civilization is state-life," I replied, curtly. But his words had set my imagination in motion. I was sitting bent over the record and visualized myself as a sort of controller and judging critic. Actually, my rapacious imagination was seeking in the most distant, the most unknown place, something to relieve me from the present,

131

or give me a key to unlock it. But this I did not understand.

One point in the record indeed made me sit up. The man had related a tradition about a race beyond the border who once had belonged to certain border people of the Worldstate. The district was said to have been cut in two during the great wars, and its population also.

I looked up.

"This is too much, this about the border people," I said, with a voice shaking from righteous indignation. "It is both immoral and unscientific."

"Unscientific?" he repeated, almost absent-mindedly.

"Yes! Unscientific! Don't you know, my Chief, that our biologists now consider it fully proven that we here in the Worldstate and those creatures on the other side of the border definitely spring from different species of apes, as different as night is from day, indeed, so different that one very well might ask if the neighbor 'people' ought to be called humans."

"I am not a biologist," he replied, evasively. "I haven't heard about that."

"Then I am pleased to have the opportunity to tell you. For it is indeed so. And the question of its being an immoral tradition I assume I need not go into further. You can yourself imagine the consequences of a border war. Could it be possible that this whole lunatic sect—with their teachings, customs, and life philosophy—is one link in the chain of our border-state's attempt to undermine our security, one detail of many in the immense espionage apparatus they seem to have at their disposal?"

Rissen was silent for a long time, and then said at last. "It was primarily because of that tradition he was convicted."

"I'm only surprised he wasn't condemned to death."

"He is very capable in his field, a worker in the dye factory where experts seem to be rare."

I did not reply; I felt his sympathies were on the side of the criminal. But I could not help giving him a little dig. "Well, my Chief, aren't you pleased now that we have at last got to the bottom of this and know where we have our precious lunatic sect?"

"I suppose it is the duty of a loyal fellow-soldier to be pleased," he said, with an irony I doubt I was supposed to get. "And may I ask you something in return, Fellow-Soldier Kall? Are you absolutely sure you do not in the bottom of your heart envy them their poisoned desert city?"

"Which doesn't exist, yes," I replied, laughing. Was Rissen all there? If this was a joke it was a poor joke without point.

But his question was to torture me for a long time, as so many of his words tortured me, as the whole Rissen, this ridiculous, sly, polite individual, tortured me.

With all the force at my command I pushed aside the thought of the desert city, perhaps not so much because it was improbable as because it was repulsive. At the same time both repulsive and tempting. It was against my reason to believe in such a city—even though in ruins, even though yawning with dangers from poisonous gases and bacteria, even though the asocial individuals who huddled there, seeking refuge, were pursued by fear and fright among the stones and occasionally perished from the lurking death—yet a city to which the State's power did not reach, a region outside the communion. Wherein lay the allurement of this thought? Superstition is often alluring, I thought in derision; it is a chest in which to keep one's lurking temptations like jewels: a deep female voice, a tremble in a man's voice, a moment never experienced of complete devotion, an abominable dream about personal confidence without limitations, a hope of quenched thirst and deep rest.

But I was unable to stave off my curiosity. I hardly dared ask Rissen about the lunatic sect's subsequent fate, which I was no longer involved in; I was afraid he would discern another, more positive interest in my questions than they actually had. I only dared make short, ironical remarks at the dinner table. And to these he gave short, morose replies. I said, for example, "That most dubious desert city—I suppose it is still on the moon? Or has it assumed any earthly location?"

And he replied, "So far at least no one has been able to locate it."

As I gave him a quick look I met his eyes for a second. He turned away immediately, but I had had time to read a question in them, and I felt it pierce: Are you quite sure you don't envy them their gas-impregnated desert city? He would have liked to surprise me with an envy of that sort, I felt. Although he forced me to take the initiative, I know it was he who was the attacker and tried to incite me to submission. I cursed my sick curiosity.

One more piece of information I was able to pick up, not from Rissen this time but from a female course-participant, even without my asking. She was talking about scrolls one of the arrested individuals had spoken of —thick stacks of documents with signs supposed to indicate musical notes but not at all like our printed music with alphabetical notation. They were said to look like bird-bodies behind a grill, as it were. No one could solve them, not even the dwellers lurking in the desert city, although there must be enormous collections from long ago epochs. I felt quite sure that if there was any music at all in those signs—the whole thing might be a hoax—it must be a primitive and barbaric music. Yet I had an almost wild longing to hear it solved some time, a silly dream that probably never would be fulfilled, neither for me nor for anyone else. And even if it were—in a collection of marches there could not possibly be anything new; how could one find help or any solution of a problem in more marches?

Meanwhile my home life was dull and empty. Linda and I had drawn so far apart that it did not seem worth while trying to communicate. Fortunately both of us were so busy that we seldom met.

A short time later I was called to Karrek on my free evening.

I felt relaxed as I sat in the Metro, my visiting license in my pocket; Karrek was and remained one of the points of support in my life; he had none of that contagious sickness which in Rissen frightened and excited.

Karrek received me in the parental room while his wife sat reading by a small bed-lamp in the family room. (They had no children.) The light was rather dim in our room also—this had recently become more and more common, for economic reasons—so I could not see the police chief's features, but from his motions I discerned something unusual which worried me although I was unable to put my finger on what it was. He was hardly at rest a single minute, he sat down, rose, measured the floor in steps that were much too long for the narrow space; when he was stopped by the wall he might hit it impatiently with his knuckles as if trying to push away the obstacle.

When he started to speak I noticed the same unusual excitement in his voice; it was exalted, almost hilarious, and he made hardly any attempt to hide his feelings.

"Well, what do you say now!" he began. "We've succeeded, you and I! Lavris must have persuaded Tatjo to issue that law against treasonable minds. It'll be in effect beginning tomorrow. And then—well, then it begins!"

For a moment I felt paralyzed that it actually had taken

place and that the fateful day was so close at hand. On him, apparently, it had only a pleasing effect; my own lips, however, trembled and I had to use all my power of self-control, as I replied, "I hope this is all for the best, my Chief. Sometimes I wish we had not started it. Don't misunderstand me—my reasons are purely of a practical nature. It seems to me there already is enough dirt to poke in, more even than the State can afford. We already are working overtime. Well, perhaps this can be corrected as soon as we have instructed enough helpers. But what to do with all the new accused ones? We can't have two-thirds of our population in prison!"

"Why not!" he said, joyously, punching his knuckles against the wall. "The difference isn't so great, and it'll make the payroll smaller. But seriously, there have been complaints from the finance chief in the city, and it must be the same everywhere. It means that for financial reasons we must choose among the informers; no one will be arrested any more unless the informer makes a detailed, written report about the reasons for his suspicions. This in itself will start the weeding. Furthermore, we will devote ourselves only to more prominent fellow-soldiers. We must direct all our attention to the State's security, you see. Inferior posts can be fine-combed sometime in the future, and robberies, thefts, unimportant private murders will come last. We must weed, weed, and weed, but never mind, we'll have enough to do."

He resumed his pacing and burst out laughing, that short, piercing neigh so characteristic of Karrek.

"It'll be hard for anyone to escape!" he said.

Just then he was standing in a position that let the lamplight glitter in his eyes. Lighted from below a face often looks quite frightening, and I was going through a very tense period in my life. The fact is that I grew ice-chilled when I saw the glitter in his jaguar-eyes—they

137

were so eerily close and at the same time far away, entirely beyond reach, contained in their own chill. Mostly in order to calm myself, I retorted, quietly, "I don't suppose that you too feel all fellow-soldiers walk about with a bad conscience?"

"Bad conscience?" he repeated, and neighed again. "Who cares if they have bad or good consciences. They may be as cool as cucumbers—no one will find it easy to get away!"

"Get away from being reported, you mean?"

"Report and conviction is what I mean. You understand —do sit down, Fellow-Soldier"—he approached me again and stooped over me, and I was only too happy to sink down in the chair, the way my knees kept shaking—"you understand, *if one has the right advisors and the right judge.* As it is we get advisors from different places, specialists in various fields, but one mustn't mete out stupid judgments, as you understand: an incorrigible person wouldn't be worth sending to be educated, and one on the simple side—with obsolete ways of thinking— the State must not be robbed of his work-contribution, in these days of falling birth-rate. But as I say—the field is open for the one who knows what he wants. Everything can be arranged, with the right judge."

I must admit I did not quite understand what he meant. But I hardly liked to tell him so. Instead, I nodded gravely and followed with fear in my eyes his pacing across the floor.

I felt a little embarrassed because it had grown so silent in the room; I imagined that the chief of police expected me to say something. His words about different punishments made me remember something I actually had intended to tell him.

"My Chief," I said, "there's something that surprises me

a little. The other day we had under injection a man, one of those from the gang, that dangerous sect of lunatics. He spread not only geographical rumors of utmost danger but also an insinuating legend that the creatures across the border were of the same race as some of our border-people. He also mouthed asocial songs. He was condemned to labor. Now I wonder: granted that it was right in this special instance—the case is closed and I do not criticize the verdict—but is this advisable, in principle? Obviously a prisoner, during his term, comes in contact with a great many other people, both guards as well as other prisoners. Of the prisoners some are perhaps in for only a short term, others longer; anyway, many are eventually liberated. Shouldn't one consider the poisoning they are exposed to from a person of that sort? Probably he will not have a chance to say much, that's true enough. But I have made a discovery; I ask you, my Chief, not to laugh at me, but I have noticed that from certain persons there emanates such a strong radiation from their life philosophy that they are a threat even when they say nothing. A single look, a motion from such an individual is in itself poison and contamination. My question is: can it be wise to let such an individual live? Even if he can be used for good work, and even if our population is in decline, isn't he liable to harm the State with his bare breath more than he aids it with his work?"

Karrek did not laugh. He listened carefully and did not show any surprise. When I had finished there was an expression of sly amusement on his face; he stopped walking around and sat down in the chair facing me. There he sat, immobile, but tense as if ready to spring.

"You needn't beat about the bush, my dear Fellow-Soldier," he said, slowly, in a low voice. "No one is more willing than I to regret the sad fact you refer to: that a great many fellow-soldiers have been given undue value only because the birth rate is falling. In spite of all the propaganda we are flooded with daily, our efforts in the marital bed have not shown desirable results. But what can you or I do about that? Enough of generalities and principles! Behind such statements there is always the individual case. Whom do you wish condemned to death?"

I could have sunk through the floor. His cynicism frightened me. It was indeed not Rissen only I had spoken about, but actually matters in general. What did he really think of me?

"You did me a great service when you persuaded Lavris," he went on. "One good turn deserves another, that's how one knows one's friends. You seem to have a certain type of intelligence, anyway, quite different from mine"—at this he neighed again—"therefore we can be of use to each other. You can tell me without fear: who is the one you wish condemned to death?"

But I could not reply. Until now my wishes had only been wishes, unreal and vague. I felt I must once more see them for myself in sober light before I acted.

"No, no!" I said. "My considerations really stem from principles. I do have experience with such pest-carriers."

I stopped short. Had I said too much? He sat immobile for a few seconds more, and I squirmed under his green eyes. Then he rose and hit his knuckles against the wall.

"You don't want to. You are afraid of me. And that I don't mind. But I will still do what I can for you. When you send in your report—or reports—have them well substantiated, remember that; from now on that will be the first condition, and I won't be doing the weeding. Please put a sign in one corner, this sign"—he drew a symbol on a paper and handed it to me—"then I'll do what I can. As I say, there's nothing to it if you have the right judge, and that we can manage. The right judge and the right advisors. I'm not going to give you up, and you can have plenty of use for me—even though you are afraid."

My sleep had never been very good, but lately it had become really poor. My monthly ration of sleeping pills was always exhausted before the middle of the month, and what Linda did not need of hers I used to the last one. I did not wish to see a doctor; I suspected I would then have the comment, "nervous constitution," noted on my secret card, and that would not be very pleasant, especially as I refused to acknowledge any such condition. No one could be more normal than I; my insomnia was only too natural and too understandable. Indeed, I should rather have considered it unnatural and an indication of sickness could I have slept well under the circumstances.

My nightmares, however, indicated well enough that I did not exactly desire to be examined with my own Kallocain. Sometimes I woke up in a cold sweat from horrible dreams in which I was the accused and was awaiting my injection, and the unspeakable disgrace that would follow. Rissen, Karrek, and even an occasional course-participant were the monsters in my dreams, but above all Linda. She was always my accuser, my judge, the one to threaten me with the Kallocain needle. In the beginning I would awaken with relief at seeing the real flesh-and-blood Linda beside me in the bed, but soon it seemed as if the nightly horrors were encroaching upon the wide-awake realities, so that each time my relief grew smaller, and the actual, waking Linda absorbed more and more of the nightmare's malign nature. Once I was close to telling her all about my nightly sufferings, but stopped at the last minute, recalling her ice-cold look in the dream. Afterwards I was glad not to have said anything. Nor did the suspicion that Linda secretly was on Rissen's side leave me in peace any longer. Were she to know what I thought of him, she could in the same moment become my enemy, a merciless enemy, so strong as she was. Perhaps she already was my enemy and only waited for the right moment to strike. No, it would have been my destruction had I confessed one word of this to her.

Much less would I have liked to tell about another dream which hardly could have been counted among the usual nightmares. It was a dream about the Desert City.

I was standing at the entrance to a street and knew I must walk down it—why I did not know but I felt with anguish that my welfare was at stake unless I succeeded. The houses on both sides of the street were piles of ruins, some tall as little mountains, others sunk into the earth and half-covered with sand and debris. In a few places creepers had taken root and struggled upwards on de-cayed walls, but between them bare and lifeless stretches baked under the burning noon sun. And I seemed to notice that in various places on these bare and lifeless stretches the stones exuded a thin, yellowish vapor. In other places a bluish haze shimmered over the sand, frightening me as much. I took a step, feeling my way between the poisonous evaporations, but in the same moment a gust of wind brought toward me the yellow vapors, diffusing them in a whirling motion, and I must step back so as not to get near them. Further along the street I could also see that the bluish shimmer began to rise like a transparent flame, almost closing off the whole street. I turned about, fearful that a similar explosion behind me might cut off my escape, preventing me from going either forward or back, but as yet there was no sign of this. Again I took a step forwards. Nothing happened. Still another. But then I heard a sharp report behind me, and when I turned I saw that the stone I had just stepped on was undergoing a transformation. It loosened up from inside, grew porous, and disintegrated in a moment, while I seemed aware of a faint, unpleasant odor. I felt inclined neither to go on, nor to remain where I stood, nor to turn back.

Then I heard strange sounds of voices emanating from a partly caved-in cellar door close by, overgrown with green creepers. I had not noticed it before, but I felt relief from my fright at seeing greenery thriving so near me. Someone was ascending the cracked, sunken steps, emerging into the light and beckoning me. I no longer remember how I gained the cellar entrance, perhaps in one wild leap over the dangerous stones. Anyway, I came into a decayed stone chamber without roof, where the sun shone down and grass and flowers swayed over my head. Never had a room with walls and roof intact seemed to offer so great a security. From the grass tufts there spread a fragrance of sun and earth and warm lightness of heart, and the voices were still singing, although now at a greater distance. The woman who had beckoned me was there and we embraced. I was saved, and wished to go to sleep from fatigue and relief. To reach the end of the street had suddenly become quite unnecessary. She said, "Will you stay with me?"—"Yes, let me stay!" I replied, and felt as free from all care as a child. Bending down to investigate some moisture on the ground, I noticed a clear spring running from one side to the other across the earthen floor, and it filled me with indescribable gratitude. "Did you not know that this is the spring of life," said the woman. Just then I realized it was a dream from which I must awaken, and I sought for some means whereby to retain it—so intensely that my heart started beating wildly and awakened me.

That dream, beautiful as it was, might perhaps have been even more open to suspicion than the nightmares, and I did not wish to talk about it, either to Linda or to anyone else. Not that Linda would have been jealous of the woman in the dream (certain of her features resembled the arrested woman with the deep voice, the one I have spoken of before, but she had Linda's eyes) but because it was such a definite answer to Rissen's question: Are you sure you don't envy them their poisoned desert city? So deep had Rissen's suggestion penetrated that even my dream life was under his influence. What would it help me if I defended myself by saying, this was not me but Rissen! No judge in the world would have listened to such a defense.

This was taking place in my mind before I was called to see Karrek, or before the new law had been issued, and before I had any means of defending myself other than an indefinite hope of revenge on Rissen sometime in the future.

When I left Karrek, with the knowledge that as soon as the next day I could translate my thoughts of revenge into action, I was in a terrible state of excitement. The goal, previously so distant, was suddenly within reach, but at the same time all the details involved in reaching it seemed insurmountable. If Linda really loved Rissen, wouldn't she then, in one way or another, find out that I was the accuser? How she would do it I did not know, but I was quite sure she would succeed. She would succeed, and she would take revenge. I trembled at her revenge: whatever happened I did not wish to end up under my own Kallocain.

That night I slept hardly at all. The following morning the newspaper had an article headed: THOUGHTS CAN BE JUDGED.

It contained an explanation of the new law, also a reference to my Kallocain which made it possible. And it seemed nothing could sound more reasonable than the new criminal regulations: from now on there would be no stubborn adherence to codified laws which meted out the same punishment for the hardened criminal as for the first-time offender, if caught in similar crimes. The fellow-soldier himself, not his isolated act, would be the focus of the judicial procedure. His very mind would be examined and put on record, not to answer the old meaningless question "guilty" or "not guilty," but in order to separate useful from useless material. The punishment would no longer consist of certain automatically decided years of labor, but would be carefully figured out according to the opinions of the foremost psychologists and economists as to what was worth while and what was not. A physical and mental wreck, who never could be considered of real use to the State, could not expect to be granted life on the simple defense that he had never had opportunity to do harm. On the other hand, consideration must be taken of the shortage of human material, and, if worst came to worst, even less desirable material must be spared if in spite of everything it could be used for labor. The new law against treasonable minds had gone into effect today, but at the same time it was pointed out that all accusations must be substantiated in detail, as well as signed with a certified name, not as before, anonymous; this to prevent a flood of less important accusations and a consequent drain on the State supply of Kallocain and judicially trained personnel. In any case, the police retained the right to consider or reject the reports arbitrarily.

The necessity of one's signature Karrek had not mentioned to me. This would make it still easier for Linda if she wished to sniff out Rissen's accuser.

The day passed unsensationally in my work, but I cannot say calmly and peacefully. During our dinner I did not exchange one word with Rissen. I hardly dared look at him. I had a horrid feeling he knew my thoughts and my intentions, and that he might at any moment strike and forestall me. At the same time I knew I dared not do anything, since I was not sure of Linda. Every hour's delay was dangerous, but I must delay.

Later, having supper at home, it was like a repetition of the horrible dinner. The same difficulty in meeting Linda's eyes as earlier Rissen's, the same feeling that she must know all, the same animosity charging the air between us. The seconds crept on and I thought the home-assistant would never leave and the children go to sleep. Finally I was alone with Linda, and to avoid listeners I turned up the radio full blast and placed her and myself in a position where the loudspeaker was between us and the police ear.

I do not remember now what sort of propaganda was spurting out over us from the radio. I was too occupied with my inner turmoil to notice. Not with the slightest expression did Linda show what she thought either of the lecture or of my eagerness to have her sit in just that chair; probably she had suspected what I was up to, and listened as little as I. Only when I moved my chair close to hers did she look at me inquisitively.

"Linda," I said, "there is something I must ask you about."

"Well," she said, without any sign of surprise. I had always known her self-control was perfect. And I had always known that if we two should come to the utmost and last—a fight for life or death—she would be the most

. 147

formidable antagonist. Wasn't that actually the reason I could not let her go? Wasn't I afraid of what might happen later? In my very love was the great fear; I knew it, indeed, had known it for long. But there was also a dream of security without limitation, a dream that my very stubborn love would in due time force her to become my ally. How this would come about, and how I would know that it had taken place, I had no idea; it was a dream as indefinite and as far from reality as the dream of a life after death. But what was certain was that in the next moment I could have lost this dreamed-of security. From unsure confederates we could in one minute have become bitter enemies, even without my knowing it, without a change in her features or a tremble in her voice to betray her. Yet I must go on.

"Obviously it is for purely formal reasons I ask this," I continued, and tried to smile. "I am of course sure of your answer, have never for a moment thought anything else; and even if it were true, you must realize I wouldn't care in the least. I hope you know me that well—and I know you that well."

I wiped my forehead with my handkerchief.

"Well?" said Linda, and looked searchingly at me. Her big eyes seemed like spotlights, so exposed did I feel when she turned them on me.

"Well, it's nothing but this," I said, and now I did smile quite merrily. "Have you had a love affair with Rissen?"

"No."

"But you love him?"

"No, Leo, I don't."

So far we could get and no farther. Had she said yes, I would have believed her right away—I suppose. Now that she said no, I dared not trust her for a moment. What had been the use then of asking? She had seen that I was lying, she realized I did care a great deal what her answer was. Tomorrow, or the day after, she would understand why I had asked her; perhaps already now she knew, perhaps Rissen had given her a hint about the danger threatening him. I watched her face intently, I even forgot to breathe and suddenly had to draw in air deeply. My heart almost stopped when I thought I could discern a movement, barely noticeable, a sort of shiver, yet a sign. I believed more in that sign than in all her words.

"You don't believe me?" she asked, gravely.

"Of course I believe you!" I replied, with great emphasis. If only she too would believe me! If I only could lull her into assurance, then at least the evil would not have grown worse. But I suspected she would not be fooled.

We could get no further. Already this conversation had cost me so much self-control that I was quite exhausted; and yet nothing had been gained. Never before had I felt the cleft so deep and impassable. My self-control was not sufficient to fill the rest of the evening with light talk and cheer, even though we had only one hour until both of us must go on night duty. Linda was silent too, and a creeping anxiety hovered over us, sucking at our marrow.

Finally even that hour passed.

Late at night we returned home, both tired out. Linda went to sleep; I could hear her even breathing, but I lay awake. Now and again I might sink into a sort of half dozing, but each time I started up again, with an ever sharper consciousness of danger. It could be imagination —the room was quiet and Linda slept as soundly as before. But I was close to despair. Had no one until now actually ever thought of the danger inherent in two people sleeping side by side, with no other witnesses but the police eye and the police ear on the wall? And even they were no real security: in the first place, they might not always be in use; and in the second, admittedly they could influence or avenge something that happened but not prevent it. Two people alone, night after night, year in year out, and perhaps hating each other; and if the wife should awaken, what couldn't she then do to her husband ... Suppose Linda had had access to the Kallocain...

The thought struck me as a wave tosses a piece of bark. I had no longer any choice, I must act as I had intended, in pure self-defense, to save my life. In some way I must succeed. Using some excuse I could get hold of the small amount of Kallocain needed. Linda must be forced to give up her secrets.

Then she would be in my power as I never had been in hers. Then she would never dare hurt me. Then I could also go ahead and report Rissen.

Then I would be free.

I did not sleep much that night, but by the time I left for work I had shaken off the worry and indecision that had hung heavily upon me the previous day; I was intent on action and already that was a liberation.

Nothing was simpler than to hide away enough Kallocain for one injection. Small amounts were always lost anyway during experiments, and the control-weighings took place rather seldom, especially now when urgency was interfering with our orderly ways. Moreover, it was Rissen who did the weighing; as long as he did not get a most untimely notion to surprise me today or tomorrow by checking up he would never again have the opportunity. His witness and assistant would surely never during the general confusion think of such a detail. Once tomorrow was over, then I would be safe. I must rely on my good luck and Rissen's hurry.

And so I returned home that evening with a needle in my pocket and a small bottle filled with an innocent-looking pale green fluid. And the relaxation of having taken the first step toward action gave me new strength; I was even able to keep up a joking conversation with the home-assistant and the children during supper. To Linda I only nodded, but without avoiding her look. Her eyes were spotlights but not so penetrating as what I had hidden in my pocket.

We had evening duty, and it was late before we got to bed.

I lay still for a long while and waited for her to go to sleep. When at last I felt sure I stole out of bed in the light of the little night lamp and covered the police eye. I pushed a pillow over the police ear as unceremoniously as I had seen Karrek do it. Of course it was forbidden but I had reached the edge of desperation, and whatever happened I did not wish the police to follow my activities.

I looked at Linda in the faint light, as beautiful as I seldom had seen her. With her bare gold-hued arm she had pulled the blanket up to her chin, as if attempting to cover herself even though it was very warm in the room. Her head was turned aside, projecting her fine profile against the pillow; her complexion seemed a smooth, living velvet against the heavy black brows and eyelashes. The tense red bow had relaxed in sleep, becoming a soft and very tired girl-mouth. So young she had never looked to me when awake, not even when we first got to know each other, and never so pathetic. I, usually afraid because she was so strong, was almost seized with compassion at her helpless, childlike weakness. This Linda now before me I should have liked to approach in another way —cautiously, tenderly as if we were meeting for the first time. But I knew that if I awakened her the red bow would become tense and the eyes would turn into spotlights again. She would sit up in bed, fully awake, knit her brows, and discover the cloth and the pillow on the wall. And even if I wanted to approach her, if I offered love to hide my distrust, what would be the use? A moment's illusion of belonging, an intoxication that would be dead by morning—and I still would not know where I had her as regarded Rissen.

I started by tying a handkerchief over her mouth, to prevent her from crying out in the moment of self-defense. Of course she woke up and tried to get free, but besides being the stronger I had all the advantages on my side. It was not difficult to hold her while I tied her hands and feet to keep her from wriggling away. Because I needed both my hands free.

She gave a jerk when I injected the needle but did not move afterward. She must have realized the futility of resistance.

I knew eight minutes to be the sure time for the fluid to take effect. When that time had elapsed I untied the handkerchief. In all her features I could see the injection was working; she had now almost the same girl-face she had had in her sleep.

"I know what you are doing," she said, thoughtfully, and even her voice had taken on the same childlike quality as her face. "You want to know something. What is it? There is too much you ought to know. I have too much to tell you. I don't know where to start. I wanted to myself, you wouldn't then have had to force me. But perhaps I never would have done it otherwise. It's been like that over the years; it's something I wish to say, or do, and I don't know what it is. Perhaps a lot of small matters —friendliness, coziness, caresses—and when they were impossible then the big and important matters also were impossible. One thing I know for sure: I should like to kill you. If I could only be sure it never would be discovered I would kill you. Well, what does it matter if it is discovered—I'll do it anyway. It's better than keeping on like this. I hate you because you are unable to get me out of this, I would have killed you if I hadn't been afraid. Now I dare. But not as long as I can talk to you. I've never been able to talk to you. You are afraid, I am afraid, we're all afraid. Alone, completely alone, and yet not beautifully alone as when one was young. It's horrible. I've been unable to talk to you about the children, how I've sorrowed because Ossu is away, how afraid of the day when Maryl will be gone, and Laila. I thought you might despise me. Now you may despise me, I don't care. I often wish I were a young girl again, unhappily in love instead of happily. Do you know, it is enviable to be a young girl and unhappily in love, even though one doesn't understand it then? When one is young one believes there is something else, a freedom that will come with love, a sort of refuge with the one one loves, a sort of warmth, and a sort of rest—something that does not exist. Unhappily in love—one is so blissfully in despair because just *I* did not get the great happiness with just *you*—and one believes that the others, they might have found it, it is there to be found. And you must understand, when there is such joy in the world, and all thirst has a purpose, it is not hopeless even to be unhappy. Not desperate. But happily in love— that slips away into emptiness. Then there is no purpose, there is only loneliness. And why should there be anything else, why should there be a meaning for us individuals? I have loved you too greatly, Leo, and then you were gone also. I think I can kill you now."

"And Rissen?" I asked, hoarsely, afraid the precious minutes might run out before I got to know what I wanted. "How do you feel about Rissen?"

"Rissen?" she repeated, with curiosity. "Rissen—well ... There was something special about Rissen. What was it now? He wasn't so distant as all the others. He didn't frighten anyone, and he wasn't afraid himself."

"You loved him? Do you still love him?"

"Rissen? Was I in love with him? No—no, no. If I only could have been! It was just that he was not like others, not remote. Calm. Secure. Unlike you, unlike me. If one of us had been like him—or both, Leo, both of us ... But it should have been you. That's why I want to kill you, only to get out of it, for it'll never be anyone but you, and it won't be you either."

She was getting restless, and knitted her brows. I had

not dared bring home more than one dose of Kallocain, it would have been too risky. And now I did not know what else to ask her.

"How can it be so?" she whispered in anguish. "How can it be that one seeks something that does not exist? How can it be that one is sick to death when actually completely healthy, when all is as it should . . ."

Her voice sank to a murmur, and from the greenish hue on her cheeks I deduced she was about to wake up. I supported her head and offered her a glass of water. She was still tied up, she must not have noticed it while under the influence of the injection. Now I untied her, although rather apprehensive as to what she might do when freed. During the whole procedure I had looked forward, with a mixture of worry and triumph, to the moment when she would be seized with regret and embarrassment over her enforced candor. I noticed my hand tremble, unable to hold her head quiet. Then I lowered her to the pillow again and peered uninterruptedly and anxiously at the relaxed features.

But the reaction I had expected seemed not to be forthcoming. When she opened her eyes they were very thoughtful, but as calmly wide-open as usual, and they met mine without turning away. Her mouth frightened me; the red bow failed to tauten as usual, it remained as yet resting and slack, allowing her face to retain the same childlike expression she had shown in sleep and under the injection. I did not know there could be a solemnity so frightening in its lack of self-restraint. Her lips moved perceptibly as if she were repeating her words to herself. There was nothing I could say to her, I could not disturb her, I only sat immovable and watched her face. ·

At last she went to sleep, in spite of my watching her. She slept, and I undressed silently and tried to go to sleep, too, but could not. A gnawing shame and turmoil came over me. One might have thought that I was the examined one, and not she, the way I felt. The whole time I had been quite convinced that whatever she might say she would be in my power afterwards in a different way from before, that when she awoke she would divulge secrets not to be divulged, which I could threaten to expose if she were to take a single belligerent step against me. Perhaps she had done so, I was uncertain. Her threat to kill me—I had heard similar threats many times during my work and knew they were seldom carried out. But in her case it might be incriminating—why not? It was possible that she was in my hands, it was possible that all had gone according to plan.

Except for one point: I would never be able to make use of any advantage. All she had said was said from within myself. I was sick, stirred to the bottom of my soul because she had held herself as a mirror before me. I had not suspected that she, with her tight lips, her silence, and her penetrating eyes was of the same weak timber as I. How could I threaten her, how could I force her, when this was the case.

After a brief sleep I awakened, several hours too early. Linda was still sleeping. The happenings during the night were clear in my mind the moment I awakened, but besides, there was a gnawing worry about something to be done. The next moment I knew: Rissen. Today.

Now I wished to delay the whole matter again, but could find no reason for dallying. Wasn't at least *that* problem the same as yesterday? For Rissen was the same one. It was not, had never been, because he was my possible rival that I must get rid of him. My detestation was deeper than that. Only, it seemed less urgent today, whatever the reason. But if I failed to do it now I would detest myself. Precisely now, purely by chance, I happened to have plenty of time to formulate an accusation, before Linda awakened; and *one* good thing that the happenings of the night had brought was that I knew she did not belong to Rissen, but to me.

In the weak light from the night lamp I made an outline for my report. The thorough substantiation was easy enough, the many times I had worked it out in my thoughts. Everything I had said in generalities to Karrek I repeated eloquently and convincingly. I still had plenty of time, and sitting on the bed I made a finished copy of my work, nice enough considering it was written with my fountain pen, using a chemical journal as a writing pad. Without hesitation I put my name and address below, since this was required, and on the envelop I printed the address of the police. Another three-quarters of an hour I spent in reading again and again what I had written and worrying over my new feeling of discomfort and indecision. Not until the alarm clock rang at the neighbors' and reminded me that my respite soon was up, did I put Karrek's secret sign in one corner, as I already had done many times in my imagination, put the report in an envelop, and stick the whole thing inside the journal.

Linda awakened when our alarm also went off. We looked at each other as if the night had been a dream. Before all this actually took place I had imagined an entirely different morning, with myself as victor and judge, putting down the victor's conditions to an exposed and broken Linda who was forced to surrender, completely at my mercy. But so it was not to be. We only got up, dressed, ate in silence, took the elevator together and separated outside the Metro station. When I turned about to see if she was gone I noticed she too had turned about —and nodded. I gave a start; did she perhaps after all intend to lull me into security in order to take revenge later? But for some reason, beyond common sense, I did not think so. When in the next moment she dove down into the Metro's jaws, I turned around and posted the letter.

Strange about that little secret sign in the corner. I knew Karrek sufficiently well to know that it would obliterate Rissen from the face of the earth. In the middle of the street, in the midst of fellow-soldiers hurrying to morning gymnastics and work, I suddenly stood nailed to the ground for a moment, struck with the awesome consciousness of power. Any time I could repeat my maneuver. As long as I did not collide with Karrek's own interests he would willingly sacrifice a few score lives for the service I had done him. I had power.

I have earlier spoken of the staircase I visualized as life's symbol. A rather innocent vision, although somewhat silly; the vision of an obedient schoolboy's progress from class to class, the correct official's promotion through the grades. With a touch of disgust I now suddenly felt myself standing on the uppermost platform. It was not that I lacked imagination to see myself in possession of higher degrees of power than just being in favor with the chief of police at Chemistry City No. 4. I did have imagination, I had material to build with, if I wished for greater heights and broader vistas: military promotions, the ministries of the Capital, Tuareg, Lavris. But the tiny bit of power I had in my hands just now sufficed to symbolize all. And this disgusted me.

Surely it was right, surely it was desirable that a noxious creature like Rissen be destroyed. It was not that. But I fought with doubts that one would get very far with such works of destruction, generally speaking. A day or two ago it had seemed simple enough: kill Rissen, then Rissen was removed, even the Rissen within myself, since he had been grafted there by the other one, the flesh-and-blood one. One killed Rissen and then one was a true fellow-soldier again, a happy, healthy cell in the State organism. But since then something had happened that made me less sure: the events during the night, my failure with Linda.

That it was a *failure* I could not hide from myself. True, I had obtained the information I wished—that she did not stand in the way of my decision concerning Rissen. True indeed that fundamentally I was not afraid of revenge from her, since she, when all was said and done, was as inextricably and hopelessly tied to me as I to her. True indeed that I now had her in my power, that I possessed secrets she did not wish to have divulged. True indeed all of it. Consequently it was not a failure if I only thought of the silly, limited goal I had put up for myself. And yet it was a fundamental, horrible failure in another and greater sense.

Her words about the enviable unhappy love sounded girlishly romantic, yet they contained a sort of truth which I very well could apply to my own relationship with Linda. In a way my marriage had been an unhappy love, admittedly reciprocated, but still unhappy. In a serious face, in a taut red mouth, in two severe wide-open eyes, I had dream-projected a richly secret world, which would quench my thirst, soothe my disquietude, bring me a final security for all time, if only I could find a means to enter there. And now, now I had with force penetrated as far as was possible, forced from her what she did not wish to surrender, and yet my thirst remained, my anxiety and insecurity were greater than ever. If a counterpart to my dreamed-of world existed, it was unattainable in spite of all my efforts. And like Linda I was ready to wish myself back to my enviable illusion when I had still believed that the paradise behind the wall could be realized.

What connection this had with my disgust for power I found difficult to explain, but I suspected there was a connection. I suspected that also when Rissen was killed it would turn out to be a shot into the air. In the same way as I had achieved what I attempted with Linda—obtained what I wished to know and yet failed so deeply that without exaggeration I could speak of despair—so I could also achieve what I had set my mind on with Rissen —a condemnation, and execution—and yet I should not have reached an inch nearer what I actually strove for.

For the first time in my life I had a presentiment of what power was, felt it in my hand as a weapon—and despaired.

A rumor spread through the police department; no one was sure of anything, no one had said anything definite, but all had heard it as a half-whisper, while meeting on steps or in halls without witnesses in earshot: "The Police Minister himself—Tuareg—have you heard—arrested—only a rumor—arrested for treasonable thoughts—sssh . . ."

What was Karrek thinking of this, I wondered to myself, he who was so close to Tuareg and had himself been so eager to have the new law passed? Did he know it? Perhaps it even was he . . . ?

But I had nothing to do with the rumor, I buried myself in my work.

At the dinner table I no longer avoided Rissen's eyes. If he now looked through me it would be too late anyway to ward off the blow. Moreover, I had a peculiar feeling that he was not quite real. That thing, sitting there at the table, blowing his nose in his handkerchief, almost too noisily, was a sort of mirage, a comparatively harmless reflection of an evil principle which I wished to kill. I had struck, and in the next moment the blow would fall—on the reflection. Yet, I kept trying to tell myself the reflection and the man were the same thing.

Not until I was on my way home did the soporific sensation of dreaming leave me. My feet felt heavy as I realized I must see Linda again. It was my free evening and soon we would be alone together, we two, eye to eye. I did not know how I would be able to endure it.

And then the moment had arrived. She must have looked forward to it; today it was she who pulled out the chairs and turned on the radio; but neither one of us listened to the program, as little now as then.

We sat silent a long time. I searched her face on the sly; something seemed to be working in there behind the immobility. But she said nothing. Had I after all been wrong? Were my apprehensions of the morning correct?

"Have you reported me?" I asked, in a thick voice.

She shook her head.

"But you intend to?"

"No, Leo. No, no."

Then she was silent again, and there was no question I could think of. I did not know how I could stand it. Finally I closed my eyes and leaned back in the chair, submissive before something unknown but inescapable. I found myself thinking of a young man we had had under the needle, the one who first had spoken of the secret gatherings of the lunatic sect. He had said something about the horror of being silent, how helplessly exposed the silent one is, and I understood him just now.

"I have to talk with you," she said at last, with some effort. "A long talk. You must listen. Will you?"

"Yes," I said. "Linda, I have hurt you."

She smiled, a vague, trembling smile.

"You have opened me by force, like canned goods," she said. "But it was not enough. Afterwards I realized that I must either die from shame or continue of my own will. May I continue? Do you want a little more of me, Leo?"

I could not reply, and from now on I am unable to explain what happened within me, since not the smallest particle of me did anything but listen. I have a definite impression that until that moment I had never in my life listened. What I had called listening before was essentially different from this; then my ears had functioned in their place, my thoughts in theirs, my memory registered all in detail, and still my interest had been somewhere else, I don't know where. Now, I was conscious of nothing except what she was telling me. I was absorbed in it; I *was* Linda.

"You already know something about me, Leo. You know I have dreamt of killing you. Last night, with all shame and all fear gone, I thought I could do it, but now I know I cannot. I can only dream hopeless dreams. And yet I don't think it's fear of punishment that prevents me. Perhaps I can explain it later. It is something else I want to talk to you about now. I want to talk about the children, and what I have discovered about the children. It is very long. I've never dared say anything about it. I'll start from the beginning, with Ossu.

"Do you remember when I carried Ossu? Do you remember that all the time we were sure it would be a boy? I do not know if you joined in my wish-fantasy but at least you said that you too thought it would be a boy. And you know—I think I should have been terribly insulted if it had been a girl; I would have taken it as an injustice towards me—I who was such a loyal fellow-soldier that I gladly would have died if some means had been discovered to make women superfluous. Yes, because I considered them a necessary evil—as yet necessary. I did indeed know that officially we were considered as valuable, or almost as valuable, as men—but only indirectly, only because we could bear new men, and new women too, of course, who in their turn could bear new men. And however much it hurt my vanity—one wants after all to have some small, small value, no, that isn't true, one wants to have a great, big value—however much it hurt I still admitted I was *not* worth so much. Women are

163

not as good as men, I said to myself, they don't have as great physical strength, can't lift as much, can't endure bombing raids as well; their nerves are not as useful on the battlefield; generally speaking they are inferior warriors, poorer fellow-soldiers than the men. They are only a means by which to produce warriors. To put them on an equal basis officially, that is a compliment; everybody knows it is a compliment to make them happy and helpful. Perhaps a time will come, I thought, when women prove to be superfluous, when one can salvage their ovaries and throw the rest down the drain. Then the whole State can be filled with men, and it won't be necessary to go to the expense of giving girls nourishment and education. I admit, it was a strangely empty feeling at times to know that one was only a depository, necessary for the time being, but entirely too expensive. Well, since I was so honest that I admitted it, wouldn't it have been *too* great a disappointment if, the first time I bore, I should have brought forth something that also was only a depository? But it didn't turn out so, Ossu fortunately was a man-to-be, there was almost a meaning to my being. So loyal was I in those days, Leo.

"Well, I watched him grow, and start to walk, and meanwhile I was carrying Maryl. When I stopped nursing him I only saw him mornings and evenings, before I went to work and after I got home, but it seemed so strange; my convictions on every point told me that he belonged to the State, that already he was being educated all day long in the kindergarten to become a fellow-soldier, and that the same education later would be continued in the child camp and in the youth camp. Aside from his inherited background which I knew was important—and in our case all right as far as could be checked—and which after all isn't 'our' possession since it has been inherited from other fellow-soldiers before us—I felt quite sure that his future character depended on his chiefs in the kindergarten, in the child camp, in the youth camp, on their personal examples and the rules they followed in rearing him. But I could not help but notice a great many amusing traits which I recognized from you and me. I noticed his way of wrinkling his nose and I thought: how funny—I did the same when I was little! In that way I lived again in my son. It was a proud feeling: in him I was almost growing up to be a man! And I noticed his laughter, so much like your own. In that way I almost participated in your childhood. And his way of turning his head, as you know, and something in the shape of his eyes . . . It wasn't unusual at all, but it gave me an unlawful feeling of right of possession. 'One can see he is ours,' I thought; 'our son,' I added, guiltily, for of course I knew it was not a loyal feeling. No, it was not, yet there it was. And worse, it grew stronger, and strongest of all when it concerned the unborn one I was carrying. Perhaps you remember that Maryl's birth was complicated and took a long time? I am sure this is superstition, but I imagined already then—and I have not been able to get rid of that thought—that it was caused by my unwillingness to let her leave me. When Ossu was born I was still a mother fully in the State's spirit, one bearing for the State only. When Maryl was born I was selfish, a greedy beast-female, who bore for herself and felt she had a right over what she had borne. My conscience told me I was wrong, that such thoughts were not allowed, but no feelings of guilt and shame could erase that greediness which had come to life in me. If I have any inclination to dominate—you must admit, Leo, it is not great! but it is there—it came to the fore at the time of Maryl's birth. Those short moments when Ossu was at home, it was I who decided for him, ruled over him as much as I could, if only to make me feel that he was still mine. And he obeyed, for if anything is learnt in the kindergarten it is above all to obey orders, and I knew I had the right to give orders still for a while, this being part of the State's will and the education of the fellow-soldiers. But I felt it was only pretense; my attitude toward Ossu was really *not* in the State's behalf; it was an attempt on my part to insist on all the right of possession I could get during the short time I still had him at home.

"When Maryl was born it surprised even me how calmly I took it that she was a girl, perhaps not only calmly by the way: I was even satisfied. She did not belong to the State first and foremost as a boy would have, she was more mine—she was more me, because she was a girl.

"How shall I describe what I later was to experience? As you know, Maryl is a peculiar child. She is neither you nor me. It is possible that some ancestors reappear in her —but I can't tell, it must be far back. She was simply Maryl. It sounds so simple but it was so strange. She must have seen things her own way from the beginning, even before she could speak. And later—well, you know. You know she is somehow apart.

"I noticed that my greedy hold had loosened; Maryl was not mine. For long intervals I could sit and listen as she sang to herself—or recited or whatever I might call it —fantastic dream-stories which she never had learnt in the kindergarten. From where did she get them? Fairy tales cannot be part of the mass-inheritance and come out in later generations! She had her own melody, and she did not get it from us, nor from the kindergarten. Can you understand that the thought shook and frightened me? She was Maryl. She was not like anyone else. Not a formless clay which you or I or the State only had to shape into any which pattern. Not my possession and creation. I was fascinated with my own child, in a new, shy, strange way. When she was close to me I was silent and expectant. The thought came to me that perhaps Ossu too was something in himself, although he already had gotten so far that he knew how to hide himself. I regretted that I had been so greedy about him and finally left him in peace. That time was filled with wonder and excitement and life.

"Then I discovered a new child was on the way. Nothing could be more natural, but to me it was something overwhelming. To say I was afraid is not quite true; I couldn't be afraid that something would happen to me, not of the birth or anything like that. I was stricken with fear because I felt that for the first time I could discern the incomprehensible. This would be my third child, yet I felt that never before had I known what it was to give birth. It didn't strike me any more that I was a too expensive production-machine; nor was I a greedy owner. What was I then? I don't know. One who had no say about what was happening—and yet elevated almost to ecstasy because this must happen through me. Inside me a life was coming into being—and it already had features, already character traits—and I could not change it. I was a branch that bloomed and I knew nothing about my root or trunk but I could feel the sap spring from unknown depths . . .

"I have had to talk this long, and yet I don't know if you understand me. I mean: if you understand that there is something below and behind us. That creation takes place in us. I know that this must not be said, for only the State owns us. But still I'll say it to you. Otherwise everything is without meaning."

She stopped, and I sat mute although I felt like shouting. Here is everything I have fought against, I thought as in a dream. All I have fought against and been afraid of and longed for.

She knew nothing about the lunatics and their desert city, yet she would fall under the law as inexorably as they, dreaming as she did of another communion than that of the State. Besides: I would too. Didn't I already feel this other communion, illegal and inescapable, between her and me!

I shook from head to foot. I wanted to say: Yes, yes!—It would have been a relief, as when a completely exhausted person is allowed to go to sleep. I was released from one communion which was choking me and was delivered into a new, obvious, simple one which supported but did not bind.

My lips fought with words that were not there and could not be said. I wanted to go, I wanted to act, I wanted to break everything and make everything new. There was no longer a world for me, no place to live in. Nothing except the solid communion between Linda and me.

I walked up to her, fell down on my knees on the floor, and put my head in her lap.

I do not know if any person has done so before, or will ever do so again. I have never heard it said. I only knew I was forced to, and that it contained all I wished to say and could not.

She must have understood. She put her hand on my head. We remained thus long, long.

Late in the night I jumped up and said, "I must save Rissen. I have reported Rissen."

She did not ask me any questions. I rushed to the janitor, awakened him, and asked to use the telephone; when I told him it was a call to the chief of police he made no objection.

I was unable to reach Karrek; he had given definite instructions that no one was to disturb him during the night. After many difficulties and messages here and there a sensible night watchman finally came on the phone and calmed me by pointing out that after all, no case could be settled during the night. On the other hand, if I desired to see the chief of police one hour before work in the morning, he would be glad to inform him and I might come around in time and find out if he would receive me.

I returned to Linda.

She still asked no questions. I do not know whether she understood the situation or if she was waiting for me to say something. But I could not talk, not yet. My tongue had always been a clever and dependable tool but now it simply refused to function. In the same way as I shortly before had listened for the first time in my life, I knew that if I now wished to speak it must be in a new way, for which I still was not prepared. Those particles of myself that now would have to do the talking surely had never before formed any words. Nor was it necessary as yet. I had said what I had to say—and Linda had understood me—when I put my head on her lap.

We were silent again but it was a silence of a different sort from the one that had plagued me before. Now it was only that we waited patiently together, for we had overcome our great difficulty.

Later, since neither one of us could go to sleep, Linda said, "Do you suppose there are others who have had this same experience? Perhaps among your test-persons? I must find them."

I recalled the transparent little woman whom I had shaken from her false confidence while I myself envied her. What bitter disbelief had she now reached? I thought of the lunatic sect who pretended to sleep among armed people. They must all be in prison by now.

Later she said, "Do you suppose there are more who have participated in that—that other? Who have begun to understand what it is to bear children? Other mothers? Or fathers? Or people in love? Who have not dared say what they have seen but dare when someone else dares? I must find them."

I thought of the woman with the deep voice, the one who had spoken of the organic and the organized. If she had escaped prison I nevertheless did not know where she was.

And later, from far away, as from a sea of sleep: "Perhaps a new world can come into being through those who are mothers—whether they are men or women, and regardless of whether they have borne or not. But where are they?"

Then I gave a start and was clearly awake, thinking of Rissen who all the time had known what was in me, and searched and felt for it, until I had surrendered him to death. I groaned loudly and pressed myself violently close to Linda.

One hour before work I was at the police department, where Karrek received me.

I realized what a truly friendly turn he was doing me in rising so early in order to see me, even without knowing my errand. Probably he expected something quite different from what I had to offer, information about some widespread conspiracy, or some other disclosure.

"Well—I—I put your sign on the paper," I started, stammering.

"I am not familiar with any signs," he said, smoothly and coldly. "What do you mean, Fellow-Soldier Kall?"

I realized he considered there might be witnesses. Even a police department must have wires in the walls, ears and eyes to take into account, and there must certainly be circumstances under which even a chief of police must be on his guard. I thought of the whispered rumor concerning Tuareg.

"I made a mistake," I said (as if this could be of any help!). "I mean—I mean, I've sent in a report. I wish only —I would like to get it back."

With an attitude of utmost courtesy Karrek rang and called for a stack of papers among which he searched for my report. He made me wait a long time before he looked up at me with a glint in his eye.

"Impossible," he said. "Even if the reported man weren't arrested—which he is—the police of course could not fail to consider such an extremely well substantiated report. Your petition is denied."

I stared at his face, but it was expressionless in its charged immobility. Either he was being watched, in which case he would not dare comply with my wish, especially after my insane introductory words; or I had already fallen into disgrace. What use could Karrek have of a helper who wavered!

Either way, it was impossible at the moment to speak openly with the chief of police.

"In that case," I said, "I can only ask—that—that at least he won't be condemned to death."

"It is not within my domain to decide such matters," said Karrek, coldly. "His sentence depends entirely on the judge. I can furthermore advise you that a certain judge has been assigned to this case but I have no right to give you his name, since it would clearly be a criminal offense to try to influence the judge in advance."

I felt my legs wobble under me and had to grab hold of the desk so as not to fall. Karrek did not notice it, or pretended not to notice it. In my distress I thought: if he is watched now and doesn't dare to show his old friendship, perhaps he will help me later, secretly. All this is only an act. Always before I have been able to trust him.

I straightened up, noticed Karrek smile evilly as he said with honeyed courtesy, "It might perhaps interest you to know that you have been assigned to perform the Kallocain injection in the case of Edo Rissen. You are really in line to do it since the official injector himself in this instance is under the needle. I could have asked one of the course-participants but I thought I would give you the honor."

Only later was I struck by the suspicion this was not true, that Karrek only in that moment decided to force me to participate, either because he wished to invigorate me and bring me back to order with such drastic means, or simply to torture me.

In any case it turned out as he had said. After the noon recess for dinner I was called to judicial examination in the case of Edo Rissen, and my own course-participants had to occupy themselves as best they could. Behind me I had so chaotic a forenoon that several times I had been on the verge of reporting for sick-leave. That I managed to carry on in spite of all was due to the fact that I must, that I *wished* to be present at Rissen's examination and sentencing, less in order to influence the course of the case —this I felt would be impossible—than to see and hear one last time the man I had been so afraid of and had thought I hated so deeply.

A rather large crowd had already assembled in the examination hall. I recognized a high military person who acted as judge, and the two secretaries, staring at their blank pads. Beside the judge sat people in military or police uniforms, probably special advisors in various fields —psychologists, authorities on State ethics, economists, and others—and facing these, in a rising semicircle, sat all of Rissen's own course-participants in work-uniform. At first I noticed their faces as skin-colored blobs in the conglomeration of uniforms. Then it struck me I would like to see how they reacted; with some effort I concentrated on a few faces, one after another, but they looked like masks. I released them and they dissolved into blobs of vapor as before. Just then the door opened and Rissen was brought in, handcuffed.

He looked about the room without focusing his gaze on anyone in particular, nor on me. And why should he have paid attention to me? He could not know either that I had reported him or that I absorbed every one of his motions and facial expressions in hungry despair. A glint of hope rushed through me: perhaps not only I, perhaps someone else also hid a hungry despair behind the mask? Perhaps several?

When he adjusted himself in the chair, rather casually as was his habit—sometimes he almost seemed to disappear in spite of his sturdy body, perhaps because he did not force himself on anyone any more than does an object, a tree, or an animal—he closed his eyes and smiled. It was a hopeless, rather tired smile, not meant for anyone, as if all the time he was conscious of his absolute aloneness and liked it, even seemed to be at peace with it, as I can imagine a sleepy polar-wanderer might seek his rest in the cold even though he knows it will make him go to sleep forever. And while the Kallocain took effect this helpless smile spread a sort of peace over his furrowed face; even if it had taken hours before he began to speak I could not have taken my gaze from him. Where had my eyes been before that I never had noticed what a special dignity invested this casual, unmilitary man who always had seemed rather ridiculous to me! A dignity entirely different from the stiff military dignity, because it actually was based on a complete indifference to how he looked. When he opened his eyes and began to speak I had a feeling he could just as well have been sitting in any chair, leaning back a little, staring into the brightly lighted ceiling, speaking without a drop of Kallocain in his veins, using the same words and sentences as now, because the fear and the shame that kept the rest of us back had in him been devoured by loneliness and hopelessness. I might myself have asked him to speak and perhaps he would have done so, voluntarily like Linda, purely as a gift; he would have told me all I wished to hear, about the lunatics and their secret tradition, about the desert city, and about himself, how he had been forced out into the unknown in his way, as Linda had been forced in hers—all, if I had not chosen to play enemy in my wild fear when I discovered that something forbidden in me responded to his tone in the same key and never would allow itself to be silenced again. He would have spoken at greater length then than one could persuade him to speak now, perhaps about more important matters, and have made me aware of realities within myself which I never now would discover. I had no overwhelming compassion for him because he was now to be judged and must die, but I was wild from bitterness at having maimed myself in reporting him. And I listened as hungrily as I had listened to Linda, only with greater anxiety.

I would have liked to learn something about him as a person; but he did not speak about anything personal; general topics filled him to the bursting point.

"Well, well," he said. "I'm here then. As it had to be. A question of time, to tell the truth. Are you willing to listen to the truth, you? All are not truthful enough to hear the truth, that's the sad thing. There could be a bridge between person and person—so long as it was voluntary, yes, so long as it was given as a gift and received as a gift. Isn't it strange how everything loses its value as soon as it stops being a gift—even the truth? No, of course you could not have noticed that, for then you would have seen how poverty-stricken you are, naked unto the very skeleton—and who would have the strength to see that! Who wants to see his misery, until he is forced to! Not forced by people. Forced by the vacuity and the cold—the hyperborean winter that threatens all of us. Communion, you call it—communion? Welded together? And that is what you shout from two sides of an abyss. Was there no point, not even one, a single one, in the long evolution of generations, where another path could have been chosen? Must the road cross an abyss? No time when one could have prevented the huge Tank of Power from rolling on towards emptiness? Is there a road beyond death to a new life? Is there a sacred place where fate reverses itself?

"I have wondered for years where that place might be.

If we will reach it after we have devoured our neighbor-state, or the neighbor-state has devoured us? Will roads then spring up as easily between human beings as they grow between cities and districts? Let it come soon then! Let it come—come with all its horrors! Or wouldn't even that be enough? Will the armored tank have grown so strong before that time that it no longer can be transformed from a god into a tool? Can ever a god, even if he is the deadest of all gods, surrender his power voluntarily?—I wanted so to believe there was a green depth in the human being, a sea of undefiled growing-power that melted all dead remnants in its crucible and healed and created in eternity.... But I have not seen it. What I do know is that by sick parents and sick teachers still sicker children are being brought up, until the sick has now become the norm and the healthy a horror. From lone beings are born even lonelier, from the frightened come more frightened ones.... Where might even one seed of health be hiding away, that could grow and burst through the armor?... Those poor people whom we called lunatics played with their symbols. It was at least something, at least they knew there was something they missed. As long as they knew what they were doing at least something was left. But it doesn't lead anywhere! Where can anything lead! If I should shout at a Metro station when the multitudes emerge, or at a great festival with a loudspeaker in front of me—yet my shouts would only reach a few eardrums in the million-mile Worldstate, and would bounce back as a vacuous sound. I am a cog. I am a being who has been robbed of life.... And yet: just now I know it is not the truth. It must be the Kallocain, I guess, that makes me unreasonably hopeful—everything seems easy and clear and peaceful. I am still alive—in spite of all they have robbed me of—and just now I know that *what I am goes somewhere*. I have seen the powers of death spread through the world in ever widening waves—but then must not the powers of life also have their waves, even though I have been unable to discern them? . . . Oh well—I know it is the effect of the Kallocain, but even so—why couldn't it be the truth?"

On my way to the examination hall wild fantasies had flashed through my mind—how all listeners simultaneously for some inscrutable reason would turn their attention elsewhere so that I could whisper my questions into Rissen's ear. . . . Already in the same moment I knew it was a daydream never to be realized; and quite naturally, as it turned out, not a single person, much less all at one time, turned his interested look away from Rissen. But strangely enough: even if I had had the opportunity I would have had nothing to ask. What did I care about the desert city any longer! What did I care about the traditions of the lunatics! No desert city was so well hidden and so secure as the one I now proceeded towards, and it was not miles away, in an unknown direction, but close by, very close: Linda would remain. She at least would remain.

Rissen sighed and closed his eyes, but opened them again.

"They have a presentiment!" he mumbled, and his smile turned lighter, less helpless. "They are afraid, they offer resistance—consequently they have a presentiment. My wife has a presentiment when she refuses to listen and tries to silence me. The course-participants have a presentiment when they assume their superior attitudes and consider me ridiculous. It might have been one of them who reported me—my wife or one of the students. Whoever has done it *has had a presentiment*. When I talk they hear themselves. When I move and exist, it is themselves they fear. Oh, if it only existed, that green depth, that indestructible . . . and now I believe it does exist. It must be the Kallocain, but I'm still pleased . . . that I . . . can believe it . . ."

"My Chief," I said to the judge, with a voice I tried to steady, "may I give him one more injection? He is beginning to awaken."

But the judge shook his head. "It is already quite sufficient," he said. "The case is quite clear, or what do you think, my advisors? Don't you agree with me in this case?"

The advisors concurred emphatically and withdrew with the judge to consider. Just as they reached the door to the conference room something unexpected happened. A young man among Rissen's students jumped up from his place in the rising semicircle of benches, rushed down to the podium where I was busy ministering to Rissen's discomfort at his awakening, and gesticulated wildly for the departing group to stop.

"I am the one to cause this!" he shouted, in despair. "I was the one to report on my Chief Edo Rissen! Only this morning on my way to class did I post the letter; when I arrived he was already under arrest! But all here who have heard him—all here who have heard him must realize . . ."

I intercepted the young man and put my hand over his mouth. "Be quiet!" I whispered. "You can't gain anything, you ruin yourself and save no one. Others too have reported him."

Aloud I said, "Disturbing incidents caused by persons losing their equilibrium are under no circumstances permitted while the examination is in progress. You, Fellow-Soldier on the first bench, pour a glass of water for this man. One must understand and overlook the confusion in a loyal youth who has been forced to report his chief. But calm yourself now, you need not take it so hard. You need not defend yourself publicly; you are fully justified as it is."

Greatly confused, he drank the water and stared at me. As he attempted to speak further, I silenced him brusquely and promised to speak to him after the examination was over. He slumped down on the edge of the first bench and closed his eyes. When I returned to the podium Rissen had regained his full consciousness. He sat immobile and looked straight in the air before him, still smiling to himself in his aloneness, but now his smile was bitter. Suddenly he rose from the chair, took a few wobbly steps towards the audience. I neither could nor wished to hinder him.

"You who have heard me . . . ," he began in a voice that penetrated the farthest corner, yet he was not shouting; he spoke darkly and in a low voice; until I die I will continue to hear the vibration and the intensity of his dark, low voice. Two policemen, all the time on the alert in the background, rushed forward, muzzled him, and led him back to the chair. It was deadly silent in the hall when at last the judge, followed by the advisors with measured steps, marched onto the podium to pronounce sentence. The audience rose to their feet. Rissen too was lifted to attention by the two policemen.

"A germ-carrier can be disinfected," said the judge, in a solemn, imperious voice. "But an individual who in his very bearing, through his own breath, spreads discontent with all our institutions, distrust about the future, defeatism concerning our neighbor-state's robber-attempts against our borders—such a person can never be disinfected. He is harmful to the State in whatever place or position he is and can only be rendered innocuous through death. The sentence I am about to pronounce has been arrived at, if not unanimously yet in accordance with the best advice I have received from persons appointed for their special knowledge. Edo Rissen is sentenced to death."

An awesome silence met the pronounced judgment. The young student, my fellow informer, sat stiff on his bench, pale as a sheet. Rissen, still muzzled, was taken out of the hall. As the door closed behind him I found myself standing right next to it; without being conscious of it myself I had followed him step by step as far as I could.

When I later turned about, the young man had disappeared. Since he was one of the participants in the course there would be no trouble in locating him. My thoughts mechanically kneaded a few commonplace questions: who will be the instructor of Rissen's course now? Probably one of the farthest advanced students? Who will lead my course in case I am assigned to Rissen's? Well, there are plenty of people, but actually we haven't been able to spare a single one; soon the course will finally be over, then we'll have to start a new one... It was the clatter of a mill grinding upon emptiness. I myself was in some place where it was quiet and dark.

When I returned to my own lecture hall and faced the listening semicircle—confusingly like the one I had just left, aside from judge and advisors—I had to excuse myself because of indisposition and go home. I could no longer play the comedy.

I went into the parental room, closed the door behind me, let down the bed, and threw myself on it in a sort of half-daze. The night lamp was on, the air conditioner whirred; outside the door I could hear the steps and the chores of the home-assistant. I heard the door slam shut when she went to fetch the children. Then Maryl's and

Laila's voices and noise and the home-assistant's attempts to quiet them. I heard the creaking in the service lift and the clatter of plates being set. But I did not hear Linda's voice, the only thing I was listening for.

A knock on the door made me start, and the home-assistant asked through the crack, "Do you wish your food, my Chief?"

I smoothed down my hair and went into the other room. But Linda was not there. It was already long past the usual evening meal time. Futilely I searched my memory for some duty she might be busy with—though even so she would normally come home and eat first. But I dared not show any doubt about Linda in front of the home-assistant.

"Yes, of course," I said, hesitantly, "I seem to remember she said she would be late . . . silly of me to have forgotten."

The children were put to bed and still I waited. The home-assistant left, but no Linda had shown up. In my worry I telephoned the Accident-Central, disregarding the thoughts of the janitor. There had naturally been a few accidents during the day in Chemistry City No. 4, a few traffic accidents on lines I was not familiar with, several air-conditioning failures with two deaths, and a few more cases, but all in other districts than where Linda worked.

Worst of all, I could not sit and wait any longer; my regiment was celebrating a festival that evening and I must not fail to attend except for really urgent reasons. I had been unable to perform my work, but surely I could sit and let my ears be assailed by the lecture and the speeches and the rolling of drums. If I only had known where Linda was.

She had talked about looking up people. She wanted to

contact others who had reached that so obvious communion, that belonging together. But did she know where they
were? Where had she started her search?

When it was time, I left, quite mechanically, the
thought never having entered my head that I could play
truant.

I was never to see Linda again.

It had been my intention to listen to the lecture but it was difficult. Time and again I made an attempt to collect myself, and time and again I was able to follow a few sentences. I remember this much, that it was something about the development of the state-life from the most primitive where the individual, each one a lone center, lived in permanent insecurity—insecurity in the face of nature's powers and insecurity in the face of other equally lone centers—until the accomplishment of the Worldstate which was the individual's only purpose and justification and which provided him a security without shortcomings. This ran like a red thread throughout but I would be unable to supply any details even if my life were at stake. Barely had I forced myself to attention before thoughts of Linda and Rissen and the new world that existed and wished to be heard made me forget everything around me. When I awoke from my meditations I could hardly sit still—even my sinews and muscles shouted for action. If I could not immediately move I would at any moment blow up, it seemed.

Finally I started for the exit, during the height of the lecture. The police secretary on the nearest corner platform knit his brows in disapproval, and the door guard stopped me with a questioning look. I told him my name and showed him my surface-license as proof of identity.

"Excuse me, Fellow-Soldier, but I feel very sick," I said. "I think I'll feel better if I get out in fresh air for a few minutes. I've been sick all day, been in bed, had to leave work . . ."

He wrote down my name, checked the exact time of my leaving, and then let me out.

I took the elevator up. To the gate guard I repeated my request, and here too my departure was recorded and I was permitted to leave.

I stepped out on the roof terrace.

At first I could not explain what was different out there. Something completely foreign overcame me on the vast, empty roof. I was seized with terror without knowing why. After a few moments I realized what was causing my fright: the noise of planes which usually filled the air night and day was gone. It was silent.

Down below in our living quarters and in the work rooms I had experienced a relative silence where the rumble from the Metro-network was muffled by walls and earth partitions and where the air conditioners buzzed faintly and sleepily; a reduction of all sounds, always a relief and rest, as when one feels sleep covering one with its mussel shell and one becomes alone, small and huddled up. The silence on the roof terrace was not like this relative silence; it was overwhelming.

On night marches and on my way home from lectures I had many times seen the stars twinkle among the moving silhouettes of the planes but had not paid much attention to them; they never spread enough light to make my pocket torch superfluous. I had at some time heard that they were suns far away but I cannot remember that this information had made any special impression on me. In the overwhelming silence I now suddenly beheld the universe stretching from infinity to infinity, and it made me feel dizzy to contemplate the immensity of the empty space between one star and another. An all-embracing Nothing took my breath away.

Then I heard something which I must have felt and have seen the results of, but never before have heard: the wind. A light night breeze stole along the walls and caused a faint stir among the oleanders on the roof terrace. And even though, perhaps, it spread its soft murmur over only a few blocks, I could not with all my will repel an overpowering feeling that this was the breath of the whole night-space, that it emanated from the darkness easily and naturally as when a child sighs in its sleep. The night was breathing, the night was alive, and as far out in infinity as I could see, the stars pulsated like hearts and filled the empty space with wave after wave of vibrating life.

When I became conscious of myself again I was sitting on the terrace wall, freezing, not from cold since it was a warm, almost hot night, but from a strong emotion. The wind was still wafting, although more faintly, and I knew it was not originating from the darkness in space but in the air layers close to earth. The stars still twinkled as bright as before, and I reminded myself that their pulse beats of light were an optical illusion. But it did not matter. What I perceived might be mirages—which nevertheless had lent themselves to give shape to another universe, an inner universe, where I was accustomed to encounter a dry, wrinkled shell which I called myself. I felt I had touched the living depth which Rissen had called for and Linda had felt and seen. "Don't you know that here is the spring of life," the woman in my dream had said. I believed her and I was convinced that *anything could happen.*

I did not wish to return downstairs to the festival and the lecture. Now I did not care if anyone noticed my absence. All the seething activity now taking place in thousands of festival and lecture halls underground in Chemistry City No. 4 seemed distant and unreal. I did not belong there. I was participating in the creation of a new world.

I wanted to go home to Linda. And if she weren't back, if I didn't meet her? Then I would go on, go and search for the young man who also had reported Rissen, go to Rissen's wife ... Where the young man lived I did not know, but I did have the address to Rissen's apartment; it was in the laboratory district, where I had a license and could come and go as I wished. He had said, "My wife suspects—my wife might have reported me." If she had made as desperate a resistance as I, then she too was close to understanding. First home, then to her. There was no doubt in me any longer. I was participating in the creation of a new world.

No one was in sight. As inconspicuously as possible I slid over the low wall which separated the roof terrace from the street. In the stillness my steps echoed in a strange way but it never entered my head that I would attract attention; nor did anyone stop me. Since no air force fleet interfered, the starlight was sufficient to help me find my way and I did not bother to use my torch. Although I was walking all by myself here above ground, here below the stars, I had a peculiar sensation I was not alone. As I was on my way to the unknown to seek the world's living meaning, so perhaps was also Linda on her way somewhere, I did not know to whom. And wasn't it possible that just now someone else in the Worldstate's thousands of cities was on his way as we were, or perhaps already had arrived? Wasn't it possible that millions of people were on their way, openly or secretly, with or against their wills, in the immense Worldstate? And why not also in the neighboring state? Only a few days earlier such a thought would have made me recoil, but how can one stop at a state border—even if a thousand miles distant—when one has felt that one's pulses are being driven by a heart in the cosmos?

In the distance I could hear the measured steps of the district guard, a short pause, a slight scraping each time he turned about. It was funny to hear such sounds in the open air. What did the guard in his loneliness think about the silent night? Well—what did I myself think? Now for the first time I could wonder at the cause of all this silence.

But only for a moment. I could not solve that riddle, and it was of no consequence to me. The only important thing was the errand I was pursuing.

Just then a whir rose in the distance, increasing to noise of motors; the planes were there again. And it was the previous silence that made the noise so devastating, or perhaps it never had been so intense before, I did not know. In any case, it was so deafening that I had to lean against the wall while my eardrums adjusted themselves.

The air suddenly became dark, thick and dark, but there was a teeming in the dark unlike anything I had ever experienced. Close by I felt rather than saw how actual bodies filled the air around me. I pulled out my torch and directed it straight ahead. The beam fell on a human body only a yard away. Paratroopers! Next moment at least ten stronger beams hit my face, and sturdy hands grabbed my arms.

Since I was unable to assume anything but that the air force was having night exercises, I called as loudly as I could to make myself heard above the commotion, "I'm sick! I'm on my way to the subway station. Release me, Fellow-Soldiers!"

Whether they did not hear, or had other orders, in any case they did not release me. After they had searched me and disarmed me—I was in military police uniform because of the festival—I was tied hand and foot and placed on a sort of three-wheeled vehicle which some of the men had quickly put together from light parts and which seemed to be especially intended for prisoner transport. Consequently I was fastened firmly to the back seat—not especially uncomfortable but unable to move—while one soldier jumped up on the front seat and started off.

I supposed I had involuntarily happened to become a prisoner during the air force exercises and realized that the only thing I could do was to make the best of my delay; in some way I would sooner or later reach my desired destination.

Wherever we rolled along, our headlights threw a beam a short distance before us. A quarter of an hour ago not a single person had been within sight or hearing; now people swarmed in all the streets, squares, and roof terraces, each one busily employed with a definite task. I could not help but admire the organization of this gigantic night-maneuver. And the farther we went, the farther the work had progressed. I saw wire fences being put up (would they be able to remove them also before early morning when people had to pass here on the way to work?). I saw long cables being strung, containers of various kinds being moved in different directions, guards protecting all Metro-stations and all buildings. Occasionally I also noticed a three-wheeler like ours carrying a prisoner, like me, and I wondered where they intended to take us.

The three-wheelers seemed to congregate in the square facing a large tent that had been raised on a roof terrace. Those prisoners already there—a score before me—had their feet untied but not their hands and were shoved into the tent. Just inside the door I was pushed against another prisoner who objected strenuously and loudly because he, a district guard, was being subjected to this maneuver. Who would take care of his duties meanwhile? How would he be able to defend his absence when he faced his chief in the morning? The noise from motors was considerably weaker inside the tent, the walls of which had a remarkable muffler device, making it quite possible to hear what he was saying, and I felt the soldiers around him might at least have deigned to answer him; until suddenly I heard two other soldiers exchange a few words in a completely foreign language, of which I did not understand one word: we were not at all victims of a night maneuver. We were prisoners of the enemy.

To this day I do not know how the whole thing had come about. One might imagine that the enemy slowly and methodically had infiltrated the air force, position after position, with spies, and finally had each and every plane under his command. One might also imagine a wildfire-like spread of insurrection and treason, from some cause unknown to me. The possibilities are many, all equally fantastic, and the only thing I know for sure is that no fighting took place in the air, nor did I see any on the ground. It must have been a well planned and executed surprise attack.

The prisoners were waiting in a line in the entranceway of the immense tent and were then admitted one by one to an inner compartment. There sat a high military commander, with a few interpreters and secretaries. In a heavy accent I was asked in my own language my name, vocation, grade in military and civilian life. Someone bent down and said something so low I was unable to hear it, but when I saw his face I was startled; wasn't he one of my own course-participants? I was not quite sure. The chief looked up with new interest.

"Well," he said, "so you are an inventor in chemistry?

You have made an important discovery? Do you wish to buy your life with it? Will you give us your discovery?"

For a long time afterwards I used to wonder why I had said yes. It was not from fear. I had been afraid almost all my life, I had been a coward—what does my book contain except the story of my cowardice!—but just then I was not afraid. The only feeling I had was an infinite disappointment that I never would reach those who were waiting. Nor had I any thought that my life would be worth saving under circumstances like those. Imprisonment or death seemed to me about the same just then. In both cases my road to the others was broken. When it later was made clear to me that my discovery had indeed not saved me, that my life would have been spared anyway, that a great number of prisoners was a desirable gain for the border state since there as with us the birth rate was not keeping up with the losses in the great wars —when all this was made clear to me it aroused no regret, changed nothing in my attitude. I gave them my discovery for the simple reason that I wished it to survive. If Chemistry City No. 4 were laid in ruins, if the whole Worldstate were turned into a desert of ash and stone, I wished at least to imagine that somewhere in other countries and among other people a new Linda would speak like the first one, voluntarily when someone tried to force her, and another group of frightened informers would listen to a new Rissen. This was of course pure superstition since nothing can ever be repeated, but I had no choice. It was my only faint possibility to continue where I had been stopped.

How I later was moved to a foreign city, to a foreign prison laboratory to work under guard, I have already told.

I have also related how the first years of my imprisonment were filled with anxiety and speculations. I never managed to obtain any factual information as to the fate of Chemistry City No. 4, but by and by I figured out what plan the enemy had followed. The intention must have been to release gas over all streets and prevent fresh air from reaching the lower parts of the city, until the inhabitants in despair and desperation would sneak up through the few unguarded exits, singly or in groups, and surrender to the enemy. How long the oxygen containers in the city's depth would last, and if the courage of the inhabitants was such that they preferred death to surrender, or the opposite, I did not know. It is also conceivable that the whole siege ended in failure, that assistance arrived from other parts of the Worldstate. But as I say, I have never learned. In any case, there was a possibility that Linda was alive. Perhaps Rissen, too, if they had not had time to execute him. I admit this is an unlikely fantasy, and if I consulted my reason I would undoubtedly spend the rest of my life in despair. Since I do not do so, perhaps it only shows that my instinct for self-preservation forces me to seek comfort in deception. Rissen himself had said before he was sentenced, "I know that what I am goes somewhere." I am not sure what he meant by it. But moments come to me when I sit on my bunk, with my eyes closed, and I manage to see the stars twinkle and hear the wind murmur as it did that night, and I cannot, I cannot erase that illusion from my soul that I still, in spite of all, participate in creating a new world.

CENSOR'S POSTSCRIPT

Considering the many passages of an immoral nature in the composition before us, the Censorship Department has decided to place it among the avowedly dangerous manuscripts in the Secret Archives of the Universal State. Our reluctance to destroy it is based on the assumption that its very immorality may be used by more reliable scientists as material when searching for an explanation of the mentality of those beings who occupy the country bordering ours. The prisoner who produced the manuscript and who still does chemical work under guard— now with stricter control as to his use of the State's paper and pens—must with his secretly increasing disloyalty, his cowardice, and his superstition be considered a good example of the degeneration which is so characteristic of this whole inferior borderland and which can hardly be explained except as a not yet diagnosed hereditary and incurable infection, which our nation happily has been spared, and which, should it appear to be spreading across the border, would inexorably be discovered through the very means the aforesaid prisoner once helped develop. Our admonition to custodians of this manuscript is to use the greatest caution, and we recommend to perusers utmost discrimination as well as strong confidence in the far better and happier conditions in the Universal State.

HUNG PAIPHO, *Censor*